Sea Bound

a quilting cozy

Carol Dean Jones

C&T PUBLISHING
Another Maker Inspired!

Publisher: Amy Marson

Creative Director: Gailen Runge

Acquisitions Editor: Roxane Cerda

Managing Editor: Liz Aneloski

Project Writer: Teresa Stroin

Technical Editor/Illustrator:
Linda Johnson

Cover/Book Designer: April Mostek

Production Coordinator:
Zinnia Heinzmann

Production Editor: Jennifer Warren

Photo Assistant: Mai Yong Vang

Cover photography by Lucy Glover and
Mai Yong Vang of C&T Publishing, Inc.

Cover quilt: *Sunburst*, 2017, by
Teresa Stroin

Library of Congress Cataloging-in-
Publication Data

Names: Jones, Carol Dean, author.

Title: Sea bound : a quilting cozy /
Carol Dean Jones.

Description: Lafayette, California :
C&T Publishing, [2018] | Series:
A quilting cozy series ; book 3

Identifiers: LCCN 2018003521 |
ISBN 9781617457487 (softcover)

Subjects: LCSH: Quilting--Fiction. |
Retirees--Fiction. | Ocean travel--Fiction. |
GSAFD: Mystery fiction.

Classification: LCC PS3610.O6224 S43
2018 | DDC 813/.6--dc23

LC record available at
https://lccn.loc.gov/2018003521

POD Edition

A Quilting Cozy Series

by Carol Dean Jones

Tie Died (book 1)

Running Stitches (book 2)

Sea Bound (book 3)

Patchwork Connections (book 4)

Stitched Together (book 5)

Moon Over the Mountain (book 6)

The Rescue Quilt (book 7)

Missing Memories (book 8)

Tattered & Torn (book 9)

Left Holding the Bag (book 10)

Beneath Missouri Stars (book 11)

Frayed Edges (book 12)

Dedicated to
Janice Anne Bailey Packard, whose
friendship I truly treasure. She has
always been there for me with unselfish
and caring devotion and has always been
willing to lend a hand or an ear.

Acknowledgments

The creation of this book was notably enhanced by the input of a small group of amazing friends: Janice Packard, Phyllis Inscoe, and Robin Palmer. Their suggestions, encouragement, reviews, editing, and patient support have been invaluable. My sincere appreciation goes out to all three of these special people who have freely given their time, energy, and talents.

Chapter 1

Barney's tail wagged his whole body as he tried to keep all four feet on the floor and not jump up on his favorite person. "Good dog, Barney! I missed you, too," Sarah replied as she stooped down to hug her special friend.

The light on the answering machine was blinking. Sarah hung up her sweater as she listened to the message. "Hi, Sarah. This is Vicky Barnett. We have a patient who I think could really benefit from your visits. Please give me a call."

Sarah played the message twice, wondering what Vicky had in mind. Vicky was the volunteer coordinator at the local nursing home. When Sarah first moved to Cunningham Village, she had hoped to get a volunteer assignment in the nursing home, but her initial tour of the facility had caused her to rethink her plan. She was having enough trouble adjusting to life in a retirement village, and she was afraid that spending time there would make the adjustment that much harder.

Sarah thought about that first visit to the nursing home and the environment of despair she found on the upper floors. *But that was over two years ago*, she reminded herself. Now she had friends, activities, a wonderful dog, and even a gentleman friend. She giggled at the thought. *Nearly seventy years old and I have a boyfriend!*

In fact, Sarah met Charles through Vicky and the volunteer program. Sarah had been reluctant to work in the facility back then. Even so, Vicky had thought Sarah could be helpful to a particular gentleman who had recovered from a massive stroke and was now living independently in the Village. He had been isolating himself, and he needed help getting connected to the community. Upon meeting, they both realized they had met before. Charles had been the police officer sent to her home twenty years earlier to inform her of her husband's death. Over the past two years, Sarah and Charles had developed a deep friendship from her point of view and a deep love from his.

"Well, that referral of Vicky's sure worked out," Sarah said aloud with a smile. "Perhaps I should give her another chance."

Hearing her voice, Barney assumed she was talking to him. He wagged his tail and looked deep into her eyes, hoping she was talking about treats or perhaps a walk in the park. Sarah laughed at the anticipation and love he was able to express simultaneously. "Okay, fella. Let's go for a walk." Barney ran to the kitchen and clumsily pulled his leash off the hook. He dragged it to Sarah with the buckle bouncing across the floor. Sarah snapped it on, and the two friends eagerly headed out the front door.

"Where are you going with that homely mutt?" Sophie called from her porch across the street.

"He's not homely," Sarah called to her good-naturedly, knowing Sophie didn't mean it but also knowing he had a rather straggly look about him. "Do you want to take a walk with us?" she called to Sophie.

"Surely you jest," Sophie hollered, "but stop in for tea on your way back." Sarah waved her acceptance. Sophie put her book aside and reached for her cane. "… and perhaps a big slice of cake," Sophie added to herself as she moved slowly toward her kitchen. She was having trouble moving. Her back and shoulders were hurting and her side was bruised, but that was well concealed under her shirt. Her friend Andy had asked her just that morning why she was limping so badly. She didn't tell him about her fall in the bathroom the previous day. Just like she hadn't told Sarah the week before when she fell in the parking lot getting out of her car. "It's nobody's concern," Sophie told herself as she lifted the cover off the cake plate and prepared to cut two large pieces. *Nobody's concern.*

By the time Sarah and Barney appeared at Sophie's kitchen door, they were both panting. Sophie had a pan of water ready for Barney and a glass of ice tea ready for Sarah. "Sit," Sophie said to Sarah in her usual abrupt manner, pointing toward the table. Barney sat. Both women laughed, and Sarah pulled a treat out of her pocket.

As the two women enjoyed Sophie's latest culinary creation made with her three favorite ingredients—butter, sugar, and dark chocolate—they caught up on the latest gossip and laughed at Sophie's rendition of who said what to whom at the community meeting the night before. Sophie could imitate anyone and frequently did, often right to the person's face!

"I got a call from Vicky today," Sarah began, anticipating Sophie's objections. Sophie's husband had died in the nursing home following several years of progressive deterioration.

"And …?" Sophie responded with a frown.

"She said she has a patient she would like me to visit."

"And …?"

"I know how you feel about this, Sophie, but we can't hold what happened to your husband against the people that might need us now."

"You do what you want, but you won't catch me near that place. They murdered my husband."

"Sophie, you know that isn't true." But Sarah knew there was no arguing with her. Sophie had spent many months sitting with her husband, remembering their love and their years together, while he sat wondering who it was that sat with him. She had brought in specialists trying to reach him, but he continued to disappear into the abyss of Alzheimer's. No one could stop it, but Sophie, to this day, blamed the nursing home.

Changing the subject, Sarah asked, "Didn't I see Andy and Caitlyn coming out of your house this morning?" Andy lived in the next block and was younger than Sarah and Sophie by about ten years. Andy was a gentle man with a troubled past. Earlier in the year, his fourteen-year-old daughter, Caitlyn, came to live with him. Andy and Caitlyn, who had previously been strangers, had become inseparable.

"Yes," Sophie responded. "They stopped by to see if I wanted to go out with them today. They were off to the mall to get Caitlyn's school clothes, and I guess Andy feels insecure about it."

"I think that girl can choose her own wardrobe without much help from her father. That's one independent young lady!" Sarah said with a proud smile. She thought of Caitlyn as family. Andy and Caitlyn had no relatives, and Caitlyn had immediately gravitated toward Sarah as a surrogate grandmother.

Cunningham Village was a retirement community in Middletown, a small Midwestern town. The Village had separate houses and one-story villas connected in groups of five for the independent residents. Sarah and Sophie lived across the street from one another in the villas. There were several apartment buildings with elevators and assistance for those residents who needed help with their care, and there was a nursing home for those needing total care. Sophie, who enjoyed the occasional gallows humor, would announce, "Cunningham Village offers the whole package, from active retirement living to a cemetery just a stone's throw away!"

As Sarah and Barney were saying goodbye to Sophie, a car pulled up across the street in Sarah's driveway. An unfamiliar man got out and hurried to her door. "I'd better get over there," Sarah announced. "Whoever that is seems to be in a hurry."

"Sarah Miller?" the stranger asked hesitantly as Sarah approached.

"Yes," she responded with a puzzled look. She thought she would recognize him once she got closer, but although he looked slightly familiar, she couldn't place him. She glanced back at Sophie's house and saw that Sophie was waiting at the door, protectively watching over her.

"Hi," the man said. "I'm Gary Pearson, Rose's grandson."

"Oh my! Gary! I'm so embarrassed. I didn't recognize you. What are you doing in Middletown?"

"It's no wonder you didn't recognize me," Gary responded, beaming. "It's been over twenty years since we saw each other!" They exchanged an awkward hug, and Sarah waved to Sophie that all was well. "My company needed someone to go to Hamilton to meet with some buyers. Since Hamilton is only a forty-five-minute drive from Middletown, I volunteered to make the trip so I could come see you."

"Well how sweet of you, Gary!" In a more serious tone, Sarah laid her hand on the man's arm and said, "I'm sorry about your grandmother. Aunt Rose was very special to me. I wanted to come to the funeral, but …"

"No explanation necessary, Sarah. No one expected you to make that trip. Portland is a long trip to make for just a day or two."

Gary put his arm around Sarah's shoulder, and they walked into her house. Barney ran up to meet them, but seeing Gary, he backed away and looked at Sarah. "It's okay, fella. He's one of the good guys."

Gary chuckled, and Sarah noticed how his eyes twinkled when he laughed. Sarah hadn't seen her Aunt Rose for many years, but in that moment she could see her eyes. She gave his arm a tender squeeze and asked if he would like a cup of coffee.

"I could use a whole pot of coffee, if you don't mind." He chuckled and followed her into the kitchen. "I took the red-eye and didn't get much sleep. I have a room in Hamilton, but I drove directly to Middletown as soon as I checked in so we could have a few hours together. I'll be tied up in meetings the rest of the week."

"How about a little food with that coffee?" she asked.

"If it's not too much trouble, that would be great."

Knowing he had been flying all night, she decided breakfast was in order. While he sat at the table talking about his job, Sarah fried bacon and eggs and put on a fresh pot of coffee. Barney kept his distance until they were both settled down at the kitchen table. He then cautiously checked out this new person. Before Sarah brought Barney home from the shelter, he had experienced a life on the street that Sarah didn't know much about, but she certainly noticed that he was cautious around some people.

The two cousins sat in the kitchen for a couple hours, talking about past experiences and catching each other up on happenings in their respective families. Sarah saw Gary's eyelids growing heavy. "How about a nap?" she offered.

"I'm embarrassed to say that's just what I need about now. Would you mind?"

"Not at all," Sarah responded cheerfully. "You take a nap, and when you wake up we'll plan our afternoon." Sarah led him to the guest room. She had converted it into a sewing room the previous year but had a comfortable futon for visitors. She removed a quilt and a pillow from the oak cabinet and placed them on the futon.

"What a beautiful quilt," Gary remarked. "Grandma had said you were quilting now. Did you make this one?"

"I sure did. You lie down and take a nap. When you wake up, I'll show you the few quilts I've made, and we'll decide what to do with the rest of our day."

"I have something to talk to you about, too, but we'll save that for later," Gary said, loosening his tie.

Once Gary was settled down in the guest room, Sarah hurried to the phone to return the call to Vicky.

"Hello, Vicky. It's Sarah Miller returning your call. I'm at home now if you want to call me back." *Answering machines!* Sarah knew they were necessary and often helpful, but she still yearned for the days when you called a person and you either reached them or you didn't. *So simple*, she thought.

Sarah tidied up the kitchen and took a roast out of the freezer for dinner, assuming Gary would want to stay. If he did, she thought she would invite Charles, too. She decided she would invite Charles either way. She put in a quick call to him and left him a message. *Sometimes answering machines are very helpful*, she thought with a smile.

After that was done, Sarah felt a bit at loose ends. She had planned to work on the quilt she was making, but Gary was in the sewing room. She needed to run by the fabric shop for some thread and another yard of her background fabric, but Gary was parked in the driveway and she couldn't get her car out. She was momentarily baffled, but looking down into Barney's eyes, she realized what she could do.

Sarah wrote a quick note in case Gary woke up, telling him she was out for an hour or so. She latched Barney's leash onto his collar, and again the two hurried out the door and up the street toward the nursing home. Once they reached the main entrance, however, they hesitated. Sarah wasn't sure Barney was welcome inside. She tied him to a post and stepped in to ask. She came back out a few minutes later, smiling, and told Barney happily, "You're in!"

They headed up the hall to the volunteer office. Sarah stuck her head in, holding Barney back in the hallway. "Is Vicky in?" she asked the receptionist.

"I hear a familiar voice!" Vicky came out of her office to greet Sarah. Vicky looked pleased to see Sarah and Barney. "We could use Barney here, too," Vicky said. "Have you considered getting him trained as a visitor?"

Sarah admitted she had never thought of it, but it sounded like something the two of them would enjoy. She said she would look into it.

Barney curled up at Sarah's feet as the women talked about the current assignment.

Chapter 2

When Sarah returned home, she found her cousin Gary sitting on the couch enjoying a cold beer and a baseball game. Charles sat on the nearby recliner, but he stood as she walked in. "Well hello there, stranger," he greeted. "I got your message about dinner and stopped by to respond in person, but I found this poor fellow wandering aimlessly around the house, lost and alone ..."

"Stop the dramatics!" she kidded. "I was only gone a little while. Barney and I went to the nursing home to touch base with Vicky."

"I know you folks have lots to talk about, so I'll be on my way," Charles began, "and I'll be back ..."

"No," Gary interrupted. "Why don't you stay? We'll watch the rest of the game, and tonight I'd like to take the two of you out to dinner. Would that be okay with you, Cousin Sarah?"

Sarah thought about the roast that was defrosting but decided she would cook it in the Crock-Pot the next day along with some vegetables. "Sounds good to me. You said earlier you would like to see Cunningham Village, so why don't we eat at the restaurant in the Center and we can show you around on our way there?"

"I'm game. I need to get back to Hamilton relatively early. Meetings in the morning, you know."

"Well if you eat dinner with us, you'll be on *old folk's time*. We usually eat our evening meal around 5:00, but the restaurant starts filling up at 4:30! You'll get back to Hamilton in plenty of time for a good night's sleep. You boys watch the game, and I'll pull out my quilts to show you during halftime."

"There's no *halftime* in baseball, sweetie," Charles said tenderly, hoping not to embarrass her. "But bring your quilts in whenever you're ready. The game's a dud."

Sarah was a relatively new quilter and only had a bed quilt, a throw, and a table runner to show off. She had made several other quilts that she had given as gifts: a Civil War quilt for Charles; a throw for her daughter, Martha; and a table runner she made for Sophie's seventy-fifth birthday. Most of her quilts were made in classes that she took at the local quilt shop, but lately she had been sewing on her own at home. Ruth, who owned Running Stitches (or simply *Stitches*, as her customers called it), and Ruth's daughter, Katie, were always willing to help when Sarah ran into trouble.

She stacked the quilts on a chair just inside the living room and turned to leave when Gary called to her. "Come show them to me." He picked up each piece individually and studied it. "I've been looking at quilts my whole life and can never stop marveling at the intricate, detailed work you gals put into them."

"Your grandmother's quilts were works of art," Sarah said. When Sarah was very young, her mother had been seriously ill. In those days, people didn't tell the children what was going on, and to this day Sarah didn't know what was wrong with her mother. Sarah only knew she was sent away to live with Aunt Rose for many months. To her surprise, those months turned out to be the highlight of her youth. Aunt Rose was full of wonderful stories and could make the grumpiest of people laugh. *And her quilts!* They were spectacular. Sarah had recently learned about appliqué and realized that was what made her aunt Rose's quilts so beautiful. Rose often had flowers and vines intertwined around her pieced designs.

"While we're on the subject, Sarah, I have something to talk with you about," Gary said, sounding a bit serious. Sarah noticed the twinkle had faded from his eyes.

"I think I'll run home and take care of a couple things," Charles said as he stood and turned off the television. "If it's okay with you folks, I'll be back in a couple hours."

Sarah knew he was being sensitive and giving Gary time alone with her. She wanted to object, but Gary looked as if he wanted to discuss something serious, so she simply gave Charles a kiss on the cheek and said, "See that you come back soon. I'll miss you." Charles winked and turned to leave.

"Coffee?" she asked Gary after Charles left.

"Yeah, please. Let's move into the kitchen." Gary picked up his briefcase and took it along. He placed it on the table and opened it while Sarah poured the coffee. Once she sat down with him, he took an envelope out and laid it on the table.

"Sarah, as Rose's executor, I wanted to give you this myself." She wondered why he was calling her Rose, but decided he was in a different role right now. "She left instructions," he continued, "that this was to be given to you in person. I figured I was the best person to do that, and when this opportunity to come to Hamilton came up, I jumped at it."

"I'm glad you did, Gary, but what's this all about?" He handed her the envelope, and she opened it carefully. She imagined that the smell of her aunt Rose's perfume wafted out. The note was written in her aunt's familiar handwriting, every word carefully penned.

My dear Sarah,

As I write this, I'm remembering your visit with me back in the late forties. What fun it was for me to have a young person around! As you know, it was many years later that I was finally blessed with a child of my own.

What I remember most about your time here is how enchanted you were with my quilts. You told me in your letters that you are learning to quilt, and I'm extremely happy for you. You will never be sorry.

I have chosen five quilts that I want Gary to give to you after I am gone. One of these was on your bed when you were here. The other four you will probably remember when you see them.

I want you to know that I have loved you your whole life, my dear niece.

Your aunt Rose

Sarah sat without moving. After a few minutes, she folded the letter and placed it back in the envelope. She blotted her eyes with a tissue she took from her pocket. Finally, she turned to Gary and quietly said, "I loved your grandmother very much. She was such a special person and always so good to me, and now this. It's just overwhelming. I don't know what to say."

"She knew you would give her quilts a good home," he said, feeling inadequate as men often do when faced with women's tears.

"Okay! Enough of this seriousness," Gary suddenly announced as he stood up and closed his briefcase. "I have a pile of quilts for you in the car!" Sarah jumped up, and they hurried outside. He opened the trunk and removed a large box wrapped with yards of twine. "I was glad to see there were no TSA inspection notices on this when I picked it up. I was afraid they might soil the quilts."

They returned to the house, and Gary placed the box on the kitchen table. Sarah removed the coffee cups and wiped the tabletop clean. One by one, they removed the quilts and carried each one into her bedroom, spreading it out on her bed to get the full effect. Sarah caught her breath as each one was spread out, revealing the tiny hand stitches and spectacular designs. Rose had clearly preferred soft colors— mostly pastels—but she also used the reds, blues, and violets from her garden. She had a remarkable ability to create floral designs down to the minutest detail. "Stunning," Sarah said over and over. "Absolutely stunning."

Gary started to fold them, but Sarah stopped him, saying, "Just leave them here for now. I want to look at them again before I put them away." In fact, she wanted to show them to Charles after Gary left, and she was even considering sleeping on the futon so they would be on her bed the next morning when the light was stronger.

"Granny would want you to use them, you know. She always used her quilts. All of these have been on her bed at one time or another." After they returned to the living room, Sarah noticed that Barney was patiently standing by the front door.

"I need to take Barney for a walk. Would you like to join us?" The three headed out the door and up the street toward the park. Sarah often walked through the park to get to the quilt shop. It was only a mile or so, and Barney loved the walk; he enjoyed being able to go into the shop with Sarah. Occasionally a customer would complain, but generally everyone was happy to see him.

Gary and Sarah headed to the other side of the park where there was a dog park. Once inside, Sarah unhooked Barney's leash, and he headed straight for a little white poodle with pink ribbons in her hair. They sniffed their "hellos" and began running around the periphery, yelping and gently nipping at each other. "I think your dog's in love," Gary speculated with a smile.

Sarah and her cousin sat in the park enjoying the late summer sunshine and gentle breeze while the dogs romped and enjoyed their freedom. Barney was distracted several times by squirrels and seemed to be showing off when he attempted to follow one up a tree. Pink-Ribbon Dog observed with a touch of disdain, her aristocratic nose held high. Barney's tail and head drooped as he returned to her side, seeming to be embarrassed by his lowbrow behavior.

"Time to go home," Sarah called after a while. Reluctantly, Barney returned to her side. His new friend stood by the gate watching until they were out of sight.

* * * * *

"Let's take a quick tour through the Center before we have dinner," Sarah suggested as Charles parked his car. From the outside, the Center looked like an old warehouse. In fact, it probably was in its day. Once inside, Gary expressed surprise at the transformation. There was a two-story lobby with tropical trees reaching for the skylights and two levels of rooms with glass elevators traveling between them.

Leading the small group toward the elevators, Charles explained about the various activities that went on in the Center. "We have an indoor pool for swimming and water exercise classes, an exercise room with an on-call trainer, a coffee shop …"

"… and a dance studio, a small grocery store, and a computer lab!" Sarah interjected. "In fact, I learned to use the computer there."

Charles added, "I took a woodworking class; Sarah took a hula hooping class …"

"A hula hooping class?" Gary responded with a questioning look. Sarah explained the theory around hula hooping for fitness, but he continued to look ambivalent. "It really works," she added. They continued to tour the second floor classrooms and took the elevator back down to the main floor. They walked past the pool, which had windows open to the hallway. A man and woman were swimming laps side by side, stopping occasionally and laughing together. Sarah pointed out the wheelchair parked by the ladder.

Charles winked at Sarah, knowing what it must mean to the couple to be able to romp together in the pool.

They walked to the opposite side of the building and entered the restaurant. "This is fancy! I was expecting nurses to be serving me on bed trays," Gary said jokingly as he looked across the room at the white tablecloths and candles. Their waiter, dressed in a starched shirt and black tie, took their drink orders and returned with a bottle of imported pinot grigio and an appetizer platter. Gary tested the wine and made a circle of approval with his thumb and forefinger.

After they placed their dinner orders, Sarah spoke up, saying, "Well, Charles. I have a bit of news." She proceeded to tell him about her visit with Vicky at the nursing home that morning. Gary looked surprised, expecting her to be telling him about the quilts. She was saving that story until they were alone.

Sarah went on. "Vicky has an eighty-eight-year-old patient that she wants me to visit. The woman's name is Grace, and she is in the rehab wing of the nursing home. She had a hip replacement last month and is recovering from that just fine, but she seems to be very lonely, and the doctor feels she would benefit from the volunteer visitor program."

"When will you start?" Charles asked, dipping an extra-large shrimp into cocktail sauce. Sarah told Charles she was going to meet Grace the following day just to see how they got along.

"She's a quilter," she added, "so we'll have lots to talk about!"

"You volunteer at the nursing home?" Gary asked with interest. "Isn't that pretty depressing work?" He poured the last of the wine into his glass and signaled the waiter for a second bottle.

"That's what I thought when I first went there several years ago," Sarah responded. "They took me to the Alzheimer's wing, and I withdrew from the program for a while. It was incredibly depressing. But then I had a few less stressful assignments, and in fact some of them turned out to be lots of fun." She smiled at Charles and he winked.

When they returned to Sarah's house, a storm seemed to be brewing. Sarah was concerned about Gary driving to Hamilton since he had finished most of the second bottle of wine himself. He assured her he was fine but Charles intervened. Being a retired police officer, he knew the dangers. "How would you like to take a little ride?" he asked Sarah.

"Where to?"

"I'm thinking you can drive Gary back to Hamilton, and it will give the two of you more time to visit." Sarah rolled her eyes inconspicuously so only Charles could see. Gary was a little tipsy at this point and not the best conversationalist. Charles smiled and continued, "And I will follow you in Gary's car." Sarah thought about it and realized it was the responsible thing to do. Gary *was* family. Gary balked at the idea, but Charles was able to calmly get him to agree.

On their way back home, Sarah reached for Charles' hand and gave it a gentle squeeze. "Thank you for doing that. Aunt Rose would have appreciated it, too." He returned the squeeze and smiled.

"I have something to show you when we get home," she added. Sarah told Charles about the quilts. She had placed the letter in her purse so she could read it to him on their way home. He listened attentively and said he would love to see the quilts.

When they got home, Sarah took Charles into her room and one by one lifted a quilt, only to reveal another spectacular quilt below it. Charles was fascinated by them and asked many questions, most of which Sarah couldn't answer. "I don't know much about appliqué," Sarah said, "but I'd like to learn. I wish I'd realized that while Aunt Rose was alive. She would have been an extraordinary teacher."

Before he left, Charles managed to convince Sarah to fold the quilts up so she could sleep in her own bed. She didn't put them away, however. She just folded them loosely and laid them on the futon so she could examine them in more detail the next day.

Charles didn't seem to want to leave, and being alone in her bedroom wasn't helping. Sarah knew she had to deal with her reluctance to make a commitment to this wonderful man. Charles was clearly in love with her, and she knew she loved him as well. Nevertheless, she couldn't shake the feeling that moving ahead with their relationship was somehow being disloyal to her husband's memory.

Somewhat reluctantly, she led Charles to the front door. "It's okay," he said, seeming to know what was bothering her. He gave her a gentle kiss and wrapped her in his arms in a warm hug that neither one wanted to end. Barney found it so appealing that he jumped up and nuzzled in between them. Sarah and Charles burst out laughing, and the magic moment was over.

Chapter 3

"Sarah! I'm glad you're here." The shop was bright and sunny, and Sarah could feel her creative juices flowing from the moment she walked through the door. "We just got a shipment of fabric that I know you will love!" Ruth gave Sarah a friendly hug and led her into the back room, where Katie and Anna were unpacking fabric. The bolts were still wrapped in cellophane, but the vibrant colors showed through; splashes of greens and yellows mixed with blues and violets, effervescing across the bolts.

Sarah exclaimed excitedly, "These are gorgeous!"

"They're the new Bali batiks. Aren't they scrumptious?"

"Bali batiks?" Sarah asked, looking puzzled.

"Batik is a very old technique that was developed centuries ago by the villagers and tribesmen of Malaysia and Indonesia." Ruth went on to describe the process of using melted wax to draw or paint designs on fabric and then dying the fabric. When the wax is removed, the design is revealed in the original color.

"They repeat the process over and over to get these intricate patterns of color and design," Katie, Ruth's daughter, interjected.

"Well, they are just gorgeous," Sarah remarked, gently running her hands over the bolts Katie had finished opening. Once the cellophane was removed, the colors were even more brilliant. "I will have to come up with a project."

"These are spectacular for use in an appliqué project, particularly with flowers," Katie said. "They capture the essence of a blooming garden," she added with a mischievous smile. "Or at least that's what it says on the label." They all laughed, and Katie continued to unwrap the bolts.

Sarah thought about Aunt Rose's quilts and how Rose had used various values and hues of the same color to make her flowers appear variegated. She could see how using these batiks would give the flowers depth and texture. "Maybe I should learn to appliqué," she said thoughtfully.

"I could teach you," Katie offered.

The shop was a joyful place to be. The colors, the textures, the creativity exhibited—on the walls and by the customers as they chose fabrics for their next project—were always an inspiration to Sarah. Just a little over two years earlier, she didn't know what a seam ripper was, and now it had become a good friend! And the people in this shop were responsible for teaching her a skill that she was sure would be with her the rest of her life. She thought about her aunt Rose and the beautiful quilts folded on the futon, and she wondered if someday she would be able to leave something half as beautiful to her family.

Sarah picked up the thread and the background fabric she needed as well as three fat quarters she couldn't bring herself to leave in the shop. At the last minute, she picked up a magazine lying on the checkout counter. "Is someone buying this?" she asked Katie who was getting ready to ring up Sarah's purchases.

"No," Katie responded. "I was on my way to the magazine rack to put that away. I was showing someone a picture of a basket quilt that I thought she would like to make with her 1930s reproduction fabrics, but she decided on a different pattern. Did you want it?" she asked Sarah.

"It looks interesting. I think I'll take it, too," she responded as she placed the magazine on her pile.

"That's 25% off today. You're in luck!" Katie said with a chuckle as she rang it up along with her other items.

It was almost 12:30, and Sarah headed for the nursing home to meet Grace. As she drove, she reviewed the few things she knew about the woman. Grace was in her late eighties and was getting physical therapy following a hip replacement. Medically she was doing fine, considering her advanced age. Unfortunately, she had been through the entire experience totally alone. She had no family. She had never married and had outlived her sisters. She had told Vicky that her closest friend had recently died, as well. She was alone and extremely lonely.

Sarah was feeling a bit uneasy, wondering what they would talk about and if she could really be of any help to Grace. She had learned about listening skills when she took the volunteer visitor training program the previous year. However, she was always a little nervous about making that initial connection with a stranger. *Of course, there's always the quilting*, she thought with a smile. The only other thing Sarah knew about Grace was that she was a quilter. Sarah knew that would give her an opening as far as conversation was concerned. *One day at a time, Andy always said. One day at a time.*

Sarah approached Vicky's office about ten minutes early, and the two women leisurely walked up to the second floor and through swinging doors into the rehab wing. "This wing is set aside for our patients in rehabilitation," Vicky explained. "Rehab patients are usually here temporarily, and they all have private rooms. The physical therapist and vocational therapists are in this wing, too. That door leads to a sauna and an exercise pool."

"Nice!" Sarah responded. She thought about Charles and the many months he had spent here. *He must have been lonely, too.*

When they arrived at Grace's door, Vicky knocked softly and called, "Grace, it's Vicky and the visitor I told you about. May we come in?"

"Yes, come on in," the soft voice responded.

Grace was propped up in bed, holding a book and wearing a pretty bed jacket over her gown. Her gray hair was cut short and curled softly around her face. She appeared to be a small woman, but it was hard to tell since she was covered with a quilt. *A Dresden Plate*, Sarah thought. Ruth had a Dresden Plate quilt hanging in the shop that was made by her grandmother.

Vicky introduced Sarah, explaining that Sarah was a volunteer at the Center and was learning to quilt. "I was hoping you might show her those two beautiful quilts you brought with you," Vicky added. Grace's face softened as she pulled her quilt up so it was more visible. "This is one," she said, "and the other is in the cupboard over there. Vicky?"

"I'll get it," Vicky said, reaching into the cupboard and pulling out a second quilt. Sarah came closer to the bed and studied the quilts. The second one was a Triple Irish Chain made with florals on a white background.

"These are both hand quilted," Sarah said, astonished. "Did you make these quilts?"

Grace looked proud as she smiled and responded, "Yes, I did. I made both of these ten or fifteen years ago. I haven't done much sewing lately. I have arthritis in my hands, and that slows me down."

Vicky looked at her watch and said, "Grace, do you mind if I leave Sarah here with you for a while?"

"That would be nice," Grace responded, pointing toward a chair. "Have a seat."

Sarah moved the chair closer to the bed and sat down. She looked at the Dresden Plate quilt again and examined the handwork. "This is such beautiful work," she commented. You hand appliquéd the plates to the background, didn't you?"

"Yes. I hand pieced the plates first, then appliquéd them to the background squares." The plates were primarily blue calicos with touches of mauve. The background was a mauve tone-on-tone, and Grace had used a medium blue tone-on-tone for the sashing and the border. It was completely quilted by hand.

"So much work!" Sarah exclaimed. "Do you do all your work by hand?"

"Yes. I've never tried piecing or quilting with a machine," Grace responded, fingering the lines of her quilt. "I guess I'm sort of old-fashioned," she added.

Not knowing just what to say next, Sarah decided to stay on the topic of quilts. She told Grace about the quilt shop where she had taken classes. Grace smiled as she listened and occasionally nodded her head. She was attentive but quiet at first.

Sarah was running out of things to say, so she asked Grace where she was from. Grace told her she had lived outside Middletown all her life. "My parents inherited the farm right after they were married. I think it was mid-1920. We raised our own food: eggs and chickens, milk and beef from our cows, and vegetables from our garden. We were poor but we got along."

"Tell me about your family. Did you have brothers and sisters?" Sarah asked. She knew the answer but wanted to hear about it from Grace.

Grace started talking about her sisters, Mary Sue and Maggie, and about her mother. "Mama was always working," she said with a melancholy look. "She made soap out of lard, and she canned everything we grew. She made all our dresses and matching bloomers out of flour sacks." Smiling as she thought about it, she added, "I guess that's how I got started quilting. Mama had scraps left over and she saved them in a bag. I would take a few out and sew them together until I had a small quilt." She laughed at the memory. "It must have looked terrible, but Mama always said my rag quilts were beautiful."

"And my sisters!" she added proudly. "We spent our whole lives together. They both got married, but they stayed right here. In fact, they built their homes on Papa's land and we were together until they died." Grace smiled. "I'll admit it's been lonesome without them."

Sarah wanted to know more about her sisters and their shared lives, but she decided to save something for the next visit.

"You were very lucky to have them close by for so many years," Sarah said. "So many families end up living all over the country, rarely seeing each other." *And for some people, their families live right in town and they rarely see each other,* Sarah thought, thinking of her own children, Martha and Jason.

Looking again at the quilt on Grace's bed, she said, "I would love to learn how to appliqué. Your work is exquisite." The two women talked for a while about quilts and quilting until the nurse came in to check on Grace.

After the nurse left, Sarah stood and picked up her purse, saying, "Well, Grace, it's been wonderful visiting with you. I hope you will let me come again?"

"I would love for you to come again," Grace said with a warm smile. "And I want to hear about your quilts!" Grace said, adding, "Could you bring one or two for me to see?"

With a chuckle, Sarah responded, "I will do that, but you have to promise not to laugh. Remember, I'm new at this!"

Grace had turned in the bed and had her legs hanging over the side. "Do you need help before I leave?" Sarah asked.

"No, but thank you. They have me getting up and walking a little every day. I'm just moving to that chair over there."

Sarah waited until Grace was settled in the chair and had turned on the television. "It's time for my stories," Grace said with an embarrassed giggle. "Come back soon and bring quilts!"

* * * * *

That evening, Charles and Sarah were sitting in her kitchen enjoying the pot roast meal that had been simmering in the Crock-Pot all day. Just as they were finishing their dessert and coffee, they heard a ringing from the back of the house. "Is that your cell phone?" Charles asked.

"I don't think so. It should be in my purse." She checked, and it was right where it belonged. There were no missed calls. "I thought I heard that sound several times during the night last night, but I figured I was dreaming. I didn't get up to check."

Sarah and Charles walked back to her bedroom but the ringing had stopped. It started up again just as they entered the sewing room but only rang twice before it stopped again. "It seemed to be coming from the futon," Charles said curiously.

"But there's no cell phone here," Sarah responded, lifting the quilts that were still laying on the futon. "Maybe it's under the futon. Can you pull it out?"

Charles pulled the futon away from the wall and they saw a leather cell phone case lying on the floor. Charles picked it up and pulled out the phone. "This must be Gary's phone!" he said. At that moment, it began ringing again. "Shall I answer it?" he asked, looking at Sarah. "They are certainly persistent!"

"Sure. It's probably Gary calling to see where he left it."

"Hello?"

"Where the hell have you been?" The voice was loud and angry. "I've been calling for days. Did old lady Miller go for it or not?"

Charles hesitated. This wasn't Gary calling, but it was someone obviously involved with Gary in something involving Sarah. He hated hearing his beautiful Sarah referred to as *old lady Miller*, but he had to hold his temper so he could find out more.

"Not yet," Charles responded, hoping the caller didn't realize he wasn't talking to Gary.

"Did you give her the letter?"

"Yes."

"Well …? Did she ask about the will?"

"No."

"This is like pulling teeth! *Talk to me!*" the caller demanded. "What's going on out there?"

Charles remained silent for a moment, wondering what he could say to get the man to give up information about what they were planning. Finally, he said simply, "What should I do?"

"*You're a fool!*" the caller screamed, his voice trembling with anger. "I should have done this myself," and he disconnected.

"What was that all about?" Sarah asked looking worried.

"Probably just a wrong number." Slipping the cell phone in his shirt pocket, Charles said, "I'll get it back to Gary, okay?"

Chapter 4

"May I take Barney for a walk?" Caitlyn, Andy's fourteen-year-old daughter, had stopped by to see Sarah.

They had been looking at the quilts from Sarah's Aunt Rose, and Sarah was beginning to see little hints that Caitlyn just might be interested in learning to quilt. She was asking many questions, and Sarah had been thinking about a project that wouldn't be too hard. She was considering a throw for Andy's birthday. They could make it together and Caitlyn would be learning the basics, just enough to know whether she had any interest in learning more. *It would be such fun to have a young person to teach*, Sarah thought.

"You sure may," Sarah responded. "Barney would love a walk, especially with you!" Sarah started to add that she would go, too, but decided to let them have some private time. Caitlyn had fallen in love with Barney earlier that year while she was staying with Sarah.

Caitlyn had been through a very difficult time after her mother died. Her stepfather had put her out of the house, and Andy, the father she had never met, was in prison. There was no other family, and Caitlyn had no place to go. She deck was packed with women waving pieces of fabric. Sarah laughed as she examined the picture. She sat back down to read the article.

The article was written by Stephanie Anderson, who was introduced by the magazine's editor as being well known in quilting circles for her meticulous appliqué and piecing. Being new to quilting, Sarah wasn't familiar with Stephanie, but she read the article with interest. She had never heard of a quilting cruise. As she read on, she learned it was a very popular activity among quilters. Instructors would provide instruction, patterns, and sewing machines (even project kits!), as well as a full agenda of classes, activities, and entertainment quilters would enjoy.

She wondered if the cruise lines could really fill a huge cruise ship with quilters, but as she read on, she learned that the ship would also be carrying tourists, as well as the friends and families of the quilters. There was a sample list of classes, but the article went on to give the web address and phone number for specific information and reserving a spot on one of the next six cruises. *This could be it*, Sarah thought excitedly. *This could be it!*

* * * * *

Forty miles away in downtown Hamilton, Matilda and Elwood Knowles entered an insurance agent's office, Matilda with her head held high and her back straight. She had the look of a determined woman on a mission. Elwood lagged behind, looking reticent. "Why do we have to do this? You know we can never pull it off," he said in a whiney tone that Matilda found repulsive.

"Will you just shut up!" she ordered. "We talked about this."

"*You* talked about it," he responded in a voice just low enough for her to miss most of the words.

She stopped and looked at him with her arm bent and her fist on her waist. "Would you prefer to do this on your own?" she asked with a smirk that clearly suggested she knew he couldn't do it without her.

He dropped his head and lifted his hand in a dismissive gesture, which implied he would do it her way.

They were there for over two hours. Matilda and the insurance agent worked out the details to her satisfaction.

"Two million in insurance," the agent marveled as he walked them to the door. "Here's to hoping you never need to collect it."

Matilda smiled and said, "It never hurts to be prepared!"

Chapter 5

Sarah thumbed quickly through her mail, tossing any junk into the recycle bin and placing a couple bills in the basket she kept on the kitchen counter for that purpose. She had originally planned to set up an office in the guest room, but instead she had converted it into a sewing room the first year she was living in the Village.

Sarah had intended to arrive at the nursing home mid-morning so she wouldn't interfere with Grace's afternoon television programs, but she was running a little late. She had trouble falling asleep the night before because she was filled with excitement and apprehension about her tentative decision to sign up for the quilting cruise. *Can I really afford this?*

Remembering that Grace wanted to see a couple of her quilts, she hurried to the living room and removed the throw that was neatly folded on the back of the couch. Sarah had made the throw in one of the first classes she took at Ruth's shop. It was a Log Cabin pattern in shades of peach, pale yellow, and sage with touches of brown, which exactly matched her couch.

She also took one of her aunt Rose's quilts, knowing that Grace would appreciate the fine workmanship. Hurrying out the door, she remembered that she had wanted to call Sophie and invite her to dinner that night. She had already locked the front door and didn't want to stir up Barney by going back in, so she put the quilts in the car and hurried over to Sophie's door.

"Sophie?" she called when Sophie didn't respond to her knocking. "Are you home?" There was still no response, but Sophie's car was in the driveway. Since Sophie rarely walked anywhere, Sarah decided she might be in the kitchen and couldn't hear the door. She tried the doorknob, but it was locked. She knocked again, very hard this time.

Sarah was getting worried and decided to use the key. She moved the flowerpot aside and, using the spare key hidden there, opened the door and went inside. Again, she called out. "Sophie? Are you here?"

Sarah thought she heard sounds coming from Sophie's bedroom but hesitated to walk in since her door was closed. She tapped on the door and said, "Sophie, it's Sarah. Are you in there?" She was sure she heard a response but couldn't make it out. "May I come in?" she asked. This time there was a clear response.

"Go away."

"Sophie, I can't go away. I'm worried about you. I'm going to open the door." Sarah apprehensively pushed the door open and found Sophie lying on the floor. She rushed to her and started to help her up, but Sophie let out a yelp, and Sarah realized she was hurt. "What happened?" she implored, feeling helpless. "How can I help you?"

Sophie had been partially propped up on one side, but she let herself fall back on the floor and sighed. "I hesitate to say, 'I fell and I can't get up!' because you will laugh at me."

"Sophie, do I look like I'm laughing? I have to do something, but I'm afraid to move you. I'm going to call an ambulance."

"*No!*" Sophie shouted. "Do *not* call anybody! Just give me a hand. I'm not hurt, I'm just stuck." Sophie was much larger than Sarah, but Sarah was strong. Still, she hesitated to move her until she found out what had happened and whether Sophie was injured.

"Wait here," she said to Sophie as she headed for the telephone in the kitchen.

"Where am I going to go?" Sophie replied sarcastically.

"Sorry," Sarah said on her way out of the room.

She placed a quick call to Vicky and asked her to explain to Grace she was dealing with an emergency and would try to get there later in the day or certainly by tomorrow. Then she called Charles. "Charles, I need your advice." She explained what was going on and he told her to do nothing until he got there.

"The front door is unlocked. We're in the bedroom." After a short pause, she added, "Thank you, Charles. You're always there for me." Her voice cracked ever so slightly.

"You called somebody!" Sophie yelled accusingly when Sarah returned to the room.

"I just called Charles. He will come help us figure out what to do."

"What does he know about it?" she demanded with a hint of anger in her voice.

"He's a retired police officer, Sophie. He knows what to do in situations like this. You didn't want me to call the medics, which I think is the right thing to do. So let's just let Charles come. Maybe he can help you get up."

Sophie sighed deeply and turned her face away from Sarah. After a minute or two, she spoke. "Sorry," she said softly.

Sarah got Sophie a glass of water and asked how long she had been on the floor. "I was getting out of bed and walking across the room. I don't know what happened. One minute I was walking and the next minute I hit the floor." Sarah saw that Sophie's slippers were scattered across the room and the throw rug was askew.

"Did you trip over your slippers or maybe the rug?" she asked.

"How would I know?" Sophie barked.

Deciding not to pursue the question of *how* she fell, Sarah asked gently, "Does anything hurt?"

"No ... well, not unless I move. My whole leg hurts from the hip down to my toes when I try to move. Do you suppose I broke my hip?" Sophie was starting to look worried.

"Maybe. That's why we need the medics," Sarah responded.

"But I'm so well padded! I didn't think I could ever break anything with all this nice cushioning I have." Sophie chuckled and then added, "I could sure use a nice cup of coffee." Sarah wasn't sure whether that was a good idea. If she ended up needing surgery, she shouldn't have anything in her stomach.

"Let's wait until the doctor sees you." She went on to explain her reasoning, and Sophie strongly objected to the idea of a doctor, the hospital, and surgery.

But ultimately she had no choice. The ambulance arrived at the hospital just a couple of minutes before Sarah and Charles. "You still have your flashing red light," Sarah

"Hey, Charlie! I'm glad you called!" Charles had been retired from the police department for nearly six years, but occasionally he took on special assignments for his old lieutenant. Everyone at the station called him Charlie. He never liked it much. His wife had always called him Charles, and when Sarah asked about calling him Charlie, he told her it reminded him of work and that he preferred Charles.

"I don't have much information for you," Kenny continued. "I know the call came from Portland, Oregon, but then you suspected that already. The phone belongs to Gary Pearson. There are lots of calls to and from Mason Electronics in Portland."

"Those are probably business calls. That's where he works. How about Tuesday and Wednesday of this week, including during the evening?"

"There weren't any calls going out, but there were a bunch of messages on the cell, all from someone calling himself Al. I printed those out for you, primarily just foul language. He was really hot about not reaching Gary." Kenny shuffled papers around and then added, "There was one call picked up at about 8:00 p.m. on Wednesday night. That's probably the call you told me about."

"That's it. Have any calls come in on the cell since I gave it to you?"

"Not a sound yet. I'll keep monitoring it."

"They've probably connected with each other some other way by now," Charles said offhandedly. Then he realized that if the two men had connected, they might have discussed the call he answered at Sarah's house. *This Al person, and now Gary, might realize that Sarah or someone in*

Sarah's house knew something was going on. He wondered if this might put Sarah in any danger.

"Is there any way to find out who this Al fellow is?" Charles asked.

"No, he was on a throw-away cell. But you know how to find this Gary, right?"

"Right. I'll start there. Thanks, Kenny. I appreciate what you're doing."

Just as he was hanging up, Sarah joined him. Scratching Barney's ear and watching him place his cell phone back in his shirt, she asked, "That reminds me, were you able to return Gary's cell phone?"

"No," he responded. "That's something we need to talk about."

She looked at him with curiosity as they started up the street toward the park. He simply said, "Let's grab a bench in the park and sit down where we can talk." Crossing the street, they entered the park and strolled north toward town.

It was just a little over a mile from Sarah's front door to the other side of the park and onto Main Street where Stitches, Ciara's Café, and Persnickety Place were located. Beyond these shops, there was a residential area and, beyond that, the downtown district of Middletown. Downtown was in its heyday some thirty years before Cunningham Village was even built. In those days, that was where people did their shopping; with the advent of shopping malls, Middletown's Main Street had little to offer. Even Keller's Market, where Sarah had worked for many years, had relocated near the mall.

Sarah sat down at the first bench they came to and Charles joined her. "Okay, friend," she began. "Confess. What's going on? You've been acting very strange lately."

"You're right. I've been trying to protect you, and I know how you hate that!"

"So why do you do it?" she asked in a teasing tone. "Do you just like to irritate me?" Still grinning, it hadn't occurred to her that this involved anything serious. But turning to look at him, she realized his face looked troubled. "What is it?" she asked more seriously.

Charles took a deep breath and launched into the story of the cell phone. He told her what the caller had said and what he was suspecting. He told her about his talk with Kenny. As he talked, Sarah's look changed. "What are you saying, Charles? You think Gary is up to something?" She frowned, and Charles couldn't interpret the look.

"I'm wondering," he said. "That's all. I'm just wondering if he might be involved in something."

"But why would you think it also involved me?"

Charles had chosen not to tell Sarah that the caller referred to her as "old lady Miller." It just sounded too hurtful. Instead, he said, "The caller referred to 'the Miller woman' a time or two."

"What did he say about me?"

"He wanted to know if you asked about the will," Charles responded.

"The will? Rose's will? Why would I ask about that?" Sarah seemed puzzled.

"Well, I'm wondering if you were mentioned in the will, perhaps. And maybe Gary and this other guy wanted to swindle you out of your inheritance."

"I *was* mentioned in the will. Didn't I tell you? I got a letter from some attorney, and I responded saying that I wouldn't be attending the reading. He sent me a form giving him authority to send me whatever she left me. I figured it might be a quilt or two. I remember her saying, 'This will be yours someday' when I had admired one of her quilts."

"And that's what Gary brought you?"

"Yes, the quilts—five of them."

"No money?" he asked.

"Certainly not! She wouldn't have left money to me. She had Gary, her grandson."

"Is he her only family aside from you?" Charles asked.

"Yes. The only living family. She lost her son and his wife in an automobile accident years ago. Gary was away at school when it happened. It was a very sad time."

"Sorry," Charles said and remained quiet for a minute to give her time to reflect. He then asked, "Did you actually talk to this attorney?"

"No. We communicated by mail."

"Hmm."

"Hmm? Charles, what are you thinking?"

"I'm thinking someone is attempting to dupe you out of your inheritance! Didn't Gary say he was the executor?"

"Yes, but I'm not going to accuse Gary of anything! He's family! Why would he do that anyway? He must have received the bulk of the estate, even if she did leave me something."

"Do you mind if I very quietly look into this since you don't want to? I'll be discrete, I promise."

"Okay, but don't let Gary know what you're thinking."

"May I borrow the letter you received from the attorney?"

"I didn't keep it. It was just a handwritten note anyway."

"Do you remember his name?"

"No. Sorry."

The couple continued their walk to Persnickety Place, but the mood was no longer festive. Barney led the way, but his head was low, sensing that something had changed.

Chapter 7

The two men sat on the bench outside the Portland courthouse. "Relax, Al. Everything is fine. The judge signed off on it. As far as anyone is concerned, the will has been properly executed. The Miller woman has no intention of looking into it. She is satisfied that the quilts are all that Granny left her."

Al sat frowning and looking skeptical. "What about the cell phone?"

"I lost it, okay?" Gary said defensively. "I lost it and that's all there is to it. It doesn't matter. Whoever finds it will just toss it away. I cancelled the service last week."

"But I talked to someone on the phone, and that *someone* just might get nosy."

"They don't know you or me," Gary insisted. "Stop worrying."

Al shrugged. "When will you have the money? The boss is losing his patience."

"I know, Al. Tell Giovanni the money is on the way." Gary tried to act dismissive, as if there were no problem. In fact, sweat beaded on his forehead and he could feel his shirt sticking to his back. *What if this doesn't work?* he wondered.

He owed Giovanni $80,000 in gambling debts. *How did I let this happen?*

"It's not just your neck, Gary. I went out on a limb for you. It'll be my neck, too."

Gary and Al went to school together back in the 1980s. They had been friends, but as they got older they had taken different roads. Gary went into sales, specializing in electronics. He worked for the same company for twenty-five years. He had been married for a while but lost his wife and his home due to his gambling.

Al, under his uncle's tutelage, moved into organized crime in Portland. He functioned at a low level, primarily making collections for his uncle. He had a hot temper but wasn't ruthless enough to move up in the organization. His uncle was disappointed in him and made his feelings obvious and public every chance he got.

Al was given the job of collecting his friend's gambling debts. He knew it was a test, and he knew he had to pass that test. Yet Gary was his friend. Together, they worked out a scheme that would serve them both. And that plan involved duping Gary's elderly cousin out of her inheritance.

It wasn't hard for Gary to do. Rose was his grandmother, and he was her only living relative other than her niece. *Why should Sarah get the money?* Gary felt totally justified in taking it all. But having spent some time with Sarah, he experienced a few pangs of guilt.

No one will ever be the wiser, he told himself as he and Al shook hands and walked away in opposite directions.

* * * * *

"Hi, Grace," Sarah said as she entered the room, carrying a large pile of quilts. Sarah had been visiting Grace for over a month, and they had become good friends. Grace had shared many stories from her past, including the hardships she and her family had endured during the 1930s. "Neighbors helped each other through it," Grace had said with a weak smile. "We were all in the same boat, you know." She went on to explain that the government eventually offered some help and her father was able to work part time, building roads for the Works Progress Administration. "Some people gave up and moved away, but we stuck it out," she had added proudly. Sarah had great respect for this brave, proud woman.

Grace gasped when she saw how many quilts Sarah was laying on her bed. "I thought you said you were new to quilting! How could you have so many already?" Before Sarah could respond, Grace pulled the first one open so she could see the pattern. "This is appliqué," Grace said with astonishment. "... and very skillful appliqué at that!" She looked at Sarah with amazement. "You did this?"

Sarah laughed. "No. These are the ones that Aunt Rose left to me. That one was made by her grandmother, who was born around 1850. It was probably made in the late 1800s. Isn't it beautiful?"

"And it's in perfect condition!" Grace marveled. Together they spread out the other four quilts and spent over an hour exploring the intricate designs, with Grace explaining how they were made.

"I really want to learn to appliqué," Sarah said. She went on to tell Grace about the quilting cruise and added, "This could be an opportunity for me to take classes from a master, Stephanie Anderson."

"I have two of her books," Grace exclaimed enthusiastically. "You would be very lucky to spend time with her." Grace asked about the cruise and the classes, but Sarah hadn't called to talk with the organizers yet. She was still trying to decide when she wanted to go. She was also waiting to see if Sophie might recover enough to go along.

Grace began to tire, and Sarah helped her into her bed. She transferred the quilts to a chair and asked if Grace would like to take a nap. "No, I would like for you to sit down with me. I have something I want to ask you."

"Of course, Grace," Sarah said as she pulled her chair close to the bed. "What is it?"

"I'm nearly ninety years old, and I have no family. I have no one to leave my quilts to when I'm gone."

"Grace, the doctors said you are doing remarkably well."

"I don't mean right now," she responded with a smile. She wondered why it was that people never wanted to talk about death. "But you know the day will come," she continued. "I really never gave it much thought until you brought these beautiful quilts that your aunt Rose left you and I saw how happy they made you. I want mine to make someone just as happy."

"Well you make a good point. None of us wants someone to come in and dispose of our treasures willy-nilly. I should be thinking about that, too, now that I have these quilts from Aunt Rose. So how can I help?"

"I want you to have this one, the Dresden Plate ..." As Sarah started to object, Grace said, "Stop! I'm not finished. I would like you to have the Dresden Plate, and I would like for you to look around and recommend where the others should go. We'll make the final decision together, but I need your help finding the right home for them. I don't know anyone in town, and the people I know out in the country are older than dirt," she said with a chuckle. "Maybe some young woman just taking up quilting. Or someone with a love of quilts but without the money to buy one or the ability to make one. Do you get the idea?"

"I do. And I would be very happy to come up with some ideas for you if you agree to make the final decision. How many quilts are we talking about?"

"Probably fifteen or so. Some are very old—those are the ones made by my mother and my grandmother. They are *very* old! And some are simply ones I made over the years. Wait—I guess many of those would be considered *very old* as well," she said laughing. "Will you start thinking about that?"

"I would be happy to, Grace. We have a project!" Sarah kissed her cheek and said goodbye just as Grace's "stories" started.

Chapter 8

"I noticed that you're carrying a small spiral notebook in your shirt pocket, just like a real detective. Have you been detecting?" Sarah asked Charles with a mischievous smile.

"Yes, I have been doing just that! Would you like to hear about it?"

"… If you would like to tell me," she responded playfully.

"Okay. Here goes. I contacted Mason Electronics in Portland and got your cousin Gary's personal information."

"And why did they give that information to you, a total stranger?" she asked with her eyebrows high on her forehead.

"Because I am an official *detector*," he responded.

"And they believed that?" she asked skeptically.

"Absolutely!"

"So …?" she asked.

"So he's been with the company for twenty-five years, just as he said."

"Hmm."

"I got his social, his address, and a few vital statistics. Then I called a friend of mine in Portland …"

"You have friends all over, don't you?" she teased.

"You never know when you'll need a friend," he responded. "Anyway, my friend checked this guy's financials. He's way over his head in debt. He's lost his home, overdrawn his bank accounts, and cashed in his 401(k). He's living in a rented shack in the slums of Portland and hasn't made a car payment for six months."

"How could this be?" Sarah asked, suddenly assuming a serious tone. "He has a good job and seems to be a pretty smart fellow. What's happening to his money?"

"My guess would be gambling. That's usually it when you see this kind of pattern. Gambling or drugs, and having met the guy, my guess is gambling."

"Gambling?" she responded incredulously. "So what do you think this means?"

"I think it means he has gambling debts he can't pay, and he has a plan that somehow involves you!"

"Me?" she said with surprise. "Why me?" She looked at him skeptically, realizing he was probably over dramatizing again.

"I don't know yet, but I will find out," he responded with a confident air.

"Yes, you will," she replied, resuming her previous playfulness. "… You have friends!"

Sarah was disturbed to hear that Gary had financial problems, but she didn't take this cloak-and-dagger stuff too seriously. *Charles can sniff out a crime at a child's birthday party*, she told herself as she opened the back door to let Barney out.

Charles knew Sarah wasn't taking him seriously, and he was glad. He didn't want her to worry. He was capable of worrying enough for the two of them, and he felt something was seriously wrong. Gary and the man on the phone were up to something, and he was determined to find out what before they managed to follow through with their plan.

His bigger worry was that the men might come back. *Gary knows where she lives*, he thought. *He seems relatively harmless, but that guy on the phone has a nasty temper.* Charles wondered how he could protect Sarah without actually telling her about his fears. He could just hear her now, "A bodyguard? You think I need a bodyguard?" *No, she would never go for that!*

Sarah and Barney came back in, and Charles quickly hid his concerns. He cheerfully greeted Barney, who acted as if it had been days since they saw one another. Charles tossed a toy across the kitchen. Barney skidded on his side as he ran to retrieve it. "Let's go to the dog park," Charles suggested, and Sarah enthusiastically agreed. Barney, only catching the words "Let's go," yanked his leash off the hook and ran to the front door, panting excitedly.

As Charles watched Sarah slip her sweater over her shoulders, he knew what he had to do.

* * * * *

Sarah opened her new laptop and turned it on, unsure of its ability to work without being plugged in anywhere. "Technology!" she muttered with a dubious expression when, just as Charles had assured her, everything *magically* loaded. She was able to go directly to the website listed in the cruise ship advertisement. The picture from the magazine popped up on her screen but this time with sound. She listened to Stephanie introducing the cruises and talking about the fun that the quilters were having. Stephanie talked about the classes while pictures of previous cruises scrolled across the screen. Women were holding up their finished projects and appeared to be having a great time.

Sarah clicked on the projects link and read through the list of typical classes. She saw table runners, wallhangings, and other projects that could be completed in one session. Then she saw projects with quilts, primarily throw size but with notations that bed-size kits could be purchased. *Kits?* she wondered. Sarah found a link that described the materials and learned that quilters could order the kits for the projects if they didn't want to pack all the fabrics they would need. She also learned that all tools, including the sewing machines, were provided!

The more she read, the more excited she became. "I've got to do this," she said aloud. Barney's ears perked up, and he looked deep into her eyes to see if she were saying something that involved him. Sarah looked back and suddenly realized she would be leaving him behind. "Oh my, Barney! What will I do with you while I'm away?" Barney wagged his tail. She immediately thought of Charles, but she really hoped he would go with her. Sophie wasn't able to take care of a dog, and Sarah wanted her to go, too, if she would. Then she thought about Caitlyn. "Caitlyn and Andy would take care of you," she said, feeling a need to reassure Barney. Barney smiled and wagged his tail. Sarah knew he was smiling because he heard "Caitlyn."

Moving through the website, Sarah found a link that took her to the cruise schedule. The prices were higher than she expected, but she thought it would be money well spent. The prices for non-quilters were somewhat more reasonable. *Still*, she thought, *this might be out of the question for Sophie.*

Sophie never talked about money, but Sarah had noticed she was often frugal in her spending.

Looking through the scheduled trips over the next few months, Sarah found one going to Puerto Rico and the U.S. Virgin Islands. Sarah would apply for a passport, but she didn't know how long it would take. At least these ports were part of the United States and didn't require passports. *That way*, she thought, *if Sophie decides at the last minute to go with me, she won't need to rush out and get a passport.*

The Puerto Rico cruise was scheduled for early autumn, only six weeks away. Sophie's cast was coming off in another three weeks, but she would be using a walker for a while beyond that. *That shouldn't be a problem*, she reassured herself. She turned quickly to the special needs section of the website and learned that the ship offered rooms with wheelchair accessibility, so using a walker should be no problem at all. Public areas were accessible and there would be elevators between decks. *Sounds perfect!* she assured herself.

Moving back to the October cruise, she began reading about the projects. With eleven days at sea, there would be the possibility of nine days of classes, and a few classes were listed as only half-day sessions. Many of the kits that were being offered included batiks. Sarah was particularly interested in batiks, especially after seeing the ones that Ruth was carrying. There were also several appliqué classes taught by Stephanie. *Just what I want!* Sarah thought.

Sarah printed out the schedule so she could make some tentative choices. After changing her mind many times, she finally ended up with a list of five projects that interested her. Two were wallhangings, one involved paper piecing (which she knew nothing about), and the other was appliqué taught by Stephanie. She also chose a small throw with island colors that she felt would perk up her living room in the summer.

Another class that she went back and forth on was a quilted tote bag. She had never thought about sewing anything other than quilts, but this bag with its colorful tropical birds would be a nice reminder of the trip. Another class she was considering was a machine quilting class. It was only a half day, and she thought she would probably do it just for the exposure. Kimberly and her sister from the quilt club had a longarm quilting machine and had been doing Sarah's quilting. That was working out well for her, but it might be nice to be able to quilt the smaller items that she made herself.

She added up the additional kit charges and realized that would add another $300 or $400 to her total. She wondered if she should talk to Ruth about taking her own fabrics, but the more she thought about it the more she realized it was the fabrics that were attracting her. She thought it might be fun to have someone else choose her fabrics. It was so easy to fall into a fabric rut. So far, most of her quilts were in shades of rose, green, and brown. "This will force me out of the box!" she said to Barney. Barney heard the word "out" and ran to the front door. Laughing, Sarah turned the computer off and set her tentative schedule aside for the time being.

"Let's go talk to Sophie," she said to Barney, snapping his leash onto his collar and opening the front door.

Chapter 9

Flying over the Rockies, Charles was beginning to wish he had been more open with Sarah about his plans. He had told her he would be out of town for a few days and didn't offer an explanation. She assumed he was traveling to Colorado to visit his son, and he didn't correct her misconception. Now he was feeling guilty.

Once they were on the ground at Portland International Airport, Charles pulled out his cell phone and dialed Sarah, but there was no answer. He didn't leave a message. Charles took the escalator down to the lower level, headed for the garage where he rented a car. Driving the thirty or so minutes into downtown Portland, Charles reviewed his plan.

Using the onboard GPS, Charles drove first to Gary Pearson's home address. As he expected, no one was home. He walked around the perimeter of the house, noting an open window on the alley side of the house. He made a mental note and returned to the car.

From there, he drove the eight miles to Mason Electronics. Calling from the lobby, Charles attempted to make an appointment with Pearson. The secretary asked about the nature of Charles' business with Pearson, and after Charles told her it was personal, she put him on hold. When she returned, she said Mr. Pearson was in meetings and couldn't see him until 4:30. Charles walked through the lobby, checking security cameras and looking at the general layout. There was no security guard at the desk; Charles assumed the desk was covered only after hours.

Driving back to the Pearson house, he noted the time and decided to do a quick search of the house. He was momentarily glad he was no longer on the force, as he would be required to justify the need for a search warrant. He was strictly on a fishing expedition.

Charles drove the rental car up the alley that ran behind the houses. He looked around as he opened the back gate and entered the enclosure. He walked up to the door and knocked loudly but got no response. He went around to the front and again knocked. Still no response. Returning to the backyard enclosure, he went over to the window that was open and slipped the screen out. He pushed the window all the way up and stepped over the windowsill.

Charles found himself in a sparsely furnished bedroom containing a single unmade bed and a chest of drawers. He quietly opened the drawers one at a time, checking under and among the clothing items. He ran his hand over the underside of each drawer where people sometimes taped items they wanted to hide. He found nothing. He started to open the closet but decided to save it for later.

The bedroom door was closed, and Charles opened it just enough to get a look into the next room. The door creaked slightly, startling him. Charles stopped immediately and remained quiet. Nothing moved in the house, so he continued to open the door and look around the next room, which appeared to be a living room / kitchen combo. Charles proceeded to make a careful, in-depth search but was disappointed to find that there was nothing unusual in the small living room or kitchen. Like the bedroom, the living room was sparsely furnished. There was an upholstered couch and a chair, both well worn and soiled. There was a chrome kitchen table and two chairs in the corner of the room and a small kitchen alcove by the back door.

Charles found very little in the way of personal items, indicating that Gary was probably there temporarily, possibly on the run. Before leaving, he returned to the bedroom to search the closet. Opening the door, he found two suits and several pair of slacks. A robe hung on the hook inside the door. There was a laundry basket on the floor half filled with shirts and underwear. Charles had previously found jeans and tee-shirts in the chest. On the shelf above the clothing, there was a cardboard box carefully pushed to the back corner.

Charles pulled the box out and carried it to the table in the living room. Checking his watch, he saw that it was 2:30. Assuming Gary would remain at the office until his 4:30 appointment, Charles sat down and began removing papers from the box.

When he heard the front door lock being forced, Charles ducked into the kitchen alcove and automatically reached for his gun, only to be reminded that he had to leave it home due to TSA regulations. He felt vulnerable without his weapon but was surprised to hear the intruder almost immediately turn and leave. At first, Charles felt relieved but puzzled. Then he smelled the gasoline and the smoke. The intruder had tossed in an accelerant and a match. Charles grabbed the box, stepped over the low windowsill, and hurried to the rental car, looking in all directions to ensure he was alone. He heard the screech of a car pulling away from the front of the house.

As Charles pulled out of the alley, smoke was beginning to bellow out of the one open window.

Charles put in a call to 911 and sped away.

* * * * *

At 3:00, Gary's secretary put the call through. "Sorry, Pal," Al said without identifying himself. "The boss said you needed a warning. He sent Gimp over to burn down your house." Al's voice was monotone and Gary didn't detect any sign that he was particularly sorry despite his words.

"What?" Gary screamed. "You should have stopped him! The papers are all in the house. I was supposed to collect the balance of the old lady's money tomorrow. I need those papers!"

"Too late, Pal. You are on your own from now on. I'm going to try to negotiate my way out of this mess. I'm not going down with you."

"Al, please. We can figure this out."

"Look, Pearson. You don't get it. You're a dead man." Al disconnected, leaving Gary holding the phone with sweat running down his forehead.

There was a knock at the door, and his secretary stuck her head in, starting to announce a visitor. She stopped mid-sentence and asked, "Are you okay? Are you sick?"

"I'm okay, Charlotte, but ask Parker to wait just a few minutes." Charlotte retreated and Pearson opened his desk drawer, removing his flask. He gulped down several shots of whiskey and wiped his forehead with his handkerchief. He could feel the dominos of his life beginning to fall, one against the next until they would all be scattered at his feet.

A few minutes later, the door opened again and Charles Parker walked into the office. He didn't speak but pulled up a chair next to Pearson's desk.

"Charles," Gary said simply.

"Gary."

The two men sat quietly until Gary moved a coffee mug in Charles' direction and again reached for the flask. "Drink?" he asked.

"You go ahead. You're going to need it." Charles reached into his inside jacket pocket and pulled out a folded legal document tied with a beige ribbon. Gary dropped his eyes and stared at the cluttered desktop.

"Do you want to talk about it?" Charles asked.

Gary felt a rush of anxiety. Much to his surprise, it was followed immediately by a sense of relief. "It's finally over," he said, looking up at Charles. "Tell Sarah how sorry I am."

Charles stood up and went to the door. "Come on in," he said to the detective who was waiting in the outer office. "Detective, this is Gary Pearson." Turning to Gary, he added, "… and Gary, this is Detective Henderson of Portland's Organized Crime Unit."

"Am I being arrested?" Gary asked.

"We may have a solution for you," the detective said, addressing Gary. "We want Giovanni, and we need your help." Gary cringed when he realized what was being suggested. Al's uncle was a big fish.

"I would be a dead man if I helped you," he said, but then added, "I'm already a dead man, for that matter."

"We can offer protection," Henderson said still standing. "But charges are being filed right now against you for attempted fraud. You don't have much in the way of choices as I see it."

Gary slowly stood and picked up his jacket from the back of his chair. "Let's go," he said to Henderson.

Henderson, turning to Parker said, "Judge Mathers wants to see you first thing in the morning in his chambers."

"Judge Mathers?" Charles repeated.

"Probate judge. He's straightening out this mess." Turning to Pearson, he added with a frown, "What were you thinking, trying to rip off an old lady?"

Charles cringed at hearing his beautiful love being referred to as an "old lady."

Chapter 10

"A quilting cruise?" Sophie bellowed. "You've got to be kidding. Why would I, of all people, be interested in a quilting cruise?" The two women were sitting on Sophie's front porch, enjoying the first signs of autumn.

"Because I'm going and we would have fun, that's why!" Sarah retorted. "We're encouraged to bring our friends and family because there will be something for everyone! And if nothing else you can stretch out on a deck chair and read a book."

"And how will I get around? Just look at my ankle!" Sophie asked, holding her cast-enclosed foot up for Sarah to see.

"The cast is coming off soon, and physical therapy will have you walking in no time. Besides, you can take your walker if you need it."

"They won't let me on the plane with a walker. They'll be afraid I'll dismantle it and build a gun."

"I don't think so. Besides, Charles is talking about taking the train to Baltimore. That could be fun, too."

"Humph," Sophie responded with a frown. "Sounds expensive," she muttered.

Sarah didn't respond, feeling that Sophie hadn't intended for her to overhear. *Money just might be a problem for Sophie,* she thought. Sarah wished she could offer to buy the tickets, but that was out of the question. She decided she would stop pushing the issue, knowing that if Sophie were to decide to go she wouldn't be reluctant to say so.

"I'm driving into town today to pick up a few groceries and make a quick stop at Stitches. Would you like to ride along?" Sophie began to refuse, lifting her foot up again as proof of her inability to get around. "Also," Sarah added, ignoring the foot, "I was thinking we could stop at Persnickety for ice cream."

"I'd love to!" Sophie quickly responded with a grin. "I'll grab my purse." She eagerly hobbled back into the house.

* * * * *

"Well, hello!" Ruth greeted her with a welcoming smile as Sarah entered the shop. "Is that Sophie I see out in the car? Why don't you invite her in? I have fresh coffee and donuts."

"Thanks, Ruth, but we've been running errands and her foot is hurting. She wanted to wait in the car. I just need to ask you a quick question—no shopping today!"

Ruth called to her sister, Anna, to cover the shop for a few minutes. "Let's go in the back to talk. I need coffee myself."

The two women sat down at the kitchen table that Anna had found at a yard sale. Although Ruth had decorated the shop to reflect her artistic and creative abilities, the back room and storage room had always been in shambles. Anna took on the responsibility of fixing them up so that now those rooms were as pleasant to be in as the shop. "It looks nice in here," Sarah said. "Very homey."

"Anna's been a blessing!" Ruth said, and then added, "And Geoff has the online shop running like clockwork. We tripled our sales last month!"

"Oh Ruth, that's wonderful! You must be so happy to have your family here with you."

"It's a real joy. Unfortunately, since I have help in the shop now, Katie is starting to talk about going away to school. I will miss her, but it would be terrific for her. She needs to start creating her own life."

"She's lucky to have you for a mother," Sarah said, admiring Ruth's ability to know when to let go.

Ruth smiled and said, "That's part of being a parent, too. Now tell me about your problem."

"I have an elderly friend I've been visiting at the nursing home. Grace is in her late eighties, and she has a number of beautiful vintage quilts, some made by her mother and one made by her grandmother, both probably made in the late 1800s."

"I would love to see them!" Ruth responded enthusiastically. "Is she thinking about selling them?"

"No, absolutely not," Sarah replied. Continuing, she said, "Grace also has many quilts she made herself, and they are magnificent—mostly appliqué and all hand pieced and hand quilted. I'm thinking at least some of these would be considered vintage as well, considering her age and the fact that she has quilted her whole life."

"Absolutely! When was Grace born, do you know?" Ruth asked eagerly.

"I think she said 1924," Sarah said hesitantly, trying to remember for sure.

Ruth responded, "Then many of Grace's own quilts will definitely be vintage." Looking at Sarah quizzically, she added, "... and you said there's a problem?"

"Yes," Sarah continued. "She has no family, and she is concerned about what will happen to her quilts when she passes. She has asked me to come up with a plan. I've thought and thought but don't have any good ideas. I thought maybe you ..."

"The Hamilton Quilt Museum!" Ruth announced excitedly. "The whole collection could be donated in your friend's name."

"The Grace Hargrove Collection!" Sarah squealed. "I love it! I can't wait to tell her! She will be as excited as we are!" Sarah went on to tell Ruth about Grace. "She is in the nursing home now for rehabilitation, and I don't know if she will be able to go home at some point, but I'll bet I could arrange to bring her here to meet you."

"Maybe the three of us could drive over to Hamilton so she can see the museum. They have wheelchairs, and we could tour the whole museum," Ruth suggested.

"Perfect!" Sarah said as she stood. She hugged Ruth and thanked her profusely for solving the problem that had been weighing on her mind for the past week.

Getting back in the car, she told Sophie about her conversation with Ruth. "I just wish my other problem could be solved so easily."

"What is your other problem?" Sophie asked, looking confused.

"What has become of my ..." she hesitated, and then continued, "what has become of Charles?"

Chapter 11

G race was excited for Sarah as she listened to the details of her quilting cruise. The two had been sitting across the small table from one another in Grace's room with fabric, stencils, and scissors scattered between them. Sarah was carefully piecing a Friendship Star by hand. Grace patiently watched and offered gentle guidance as Sarah learned the rhythm of hand piecing. "My stitches are still too big," Sarah complained.

"Just keep going. You will find them getting smaller as you practice. Go on with your story. The stitching will come naturally."

Sarah sighed and said, "Okay. If you say so." Looking up at Grace, she asked, "Where was I?"

"You were telling me what classes you are going to sign up for on the cruise."

"Yes. That was it. Okay, I'm thinking about taking these two wallhanging classes. One is an appliqué class with Stephanie Anderson.

"What fabrics will you use?" Grace asked.

"I'm going to use their kits. They are featuring batiks on this cruise and will use them for most of their projects."

Sarah frowned at her project and set it aside while she threaded another needle. "The second wallhanging is paper pieced."

"Paper pieced? What's that?" Grace asked looking confused.

"I have no idea," she responded and they both laughed. "The pattern is called Sunburst, and it's in the yellows and golds of the island sun." Sarah went on to tell Grace about the tote bag she was thinking about doing and possibly the throw. "Or maybe I'll do a table runner," she said hesitantly. "I guess I'm not as ready as I thought I was. I was hoping to fill out the registration form tonight."

Sarah continued to stitch, occasionally looking at Grace for reassurance. She had been working with Grace for the past week and could tell she was going to enjoy handwork. "I also need to talk to my friend Sophie. She still hasn't decided whether she wants to go with me. Last week, I told her about the money from Aunt Rose and that I was going to buy all three of us tickets."

"How did she respond to that?" Grace asked.

"She started to object, but I told her that the decision was made. If she won't go with me, I'm going to contact the cruise people and pay for a total stranger!"

Grace laughed and said, "That should do it!"

For just a moment, Grace wished she could join the quilters on the cruise, but she realized it wasn't possible. Aside from her physical condition, she felt that life on an isolated farm in the country hadn't prepared her for something as adventurous as a cruise. However, she found the idea both exhilarating and scary. She loved hearing about it and could hardly wait for Sarah to come back and tell her all the details.

Grace wished she had known someone like Sarah when she was younger. She felt she would probably have learned to set her fears aside and have adventures of her own.

Suddenly Grace remembered that she actually *did* have an adventure in her future. Her doctor had agreed that she could leave the hospital for a full day. Sarah was going to pick her up, and along with the owner of Stitches, they would take the forty-five–minute road trip to the Hamilton Quilt Museum.

Grace assumed some of her quilts might be hanging, but she had no idea there would be an acceptance ceremony featuring her and her quilts. She also didn't know that a plaque had already been prepared for the collection or that it would read, "The Grace Hargrove Collection." Ten quilts would be exhibited to begin with, including ones made by both her mother and her grandmother. She would be surprised to see that plaques had been prepared which detailed each quilt in the exhibit with the information Grace had provided to Sarah. Her doctor had privately assured Sarah that Grace would be able to tolerate the trip and the excitement. He shared with her that he was even considering releasing her to her home, assuming full-time care could be arranged.

Just in time for Grace's stories, Sarah stood to leave. They exchanged a friendly hug, and Sarah promised to return the following Monday. "Don't forget about our trip on Thursday," Sarah said as she left.

* * * * *

"What do you mean, 'Am I going?' Of course I'm going!" Sophie, in her usual outrageous manner, caught Sarah totally off guard. "I'm still invited, aren't I?" she huffed.

"Certainly! This means that both you and Charles have finally made your decisions, so it's time to buy the tickets. Do you want to go to the travel office with me this afternoon?" Sophie was walking with a cane now and was getting around very well.

"Sure, I'll go," Sophie responded. "Also, I need some cruise clothes. What do people wear on a cruise, anyway?"

"The brochure recommends casual clothes during the day. So what we wear around here will probably be fine for being on the deck."

"My pink elephant pajamas?" Sophie asked, trying to look serious.

"... But not your pink elephant pajamas. We'll need a bathing suit or two and a cover-up. The brochure recommends that we bring a smart casual outfit or two and a cocktail dress for those formal occasions."

"Formal occasions?" Sophie asked indignantly. "And exactly what does that mean?"

"There'll be a couple of formal evenings in the main dining room and some of the special shows might be formal. I think it's a good idea to have something just in case," Sarah added, realizing Sophie was going to balk at most of the recommendations.

"Humph." After a lengthy pause, Sophie sighed and said, "Maybe this is a mistake. I don't think I'm going."

"Sophie, stop! You are making too big a deal out of the clothes. We'll go shopping, and we'll each buy one dress that will work as a cocktail dress. Then we'll each get a summer-weight pantsuit or a dress for the smart casual times. I need a new bathing suit and a couple pairs of capris. Otherwise, we're probably fine."

"I guess you're right. But I'm hard to fit. Wait! I just remembered that dress I bought to wear to that cocktail party they had for the new mayor. That would be fine for my dressy dress. In fact, it just might work as a cocktail dress, too!" Sophie began to brighten up.

"See? We probably already have most of what we need. Let's go through our closets this morning and make a list of what we need. We'll go to the travel office and stop by Mulligan's Department Store this afternoon to fill in the gaps. Do you need a bathing suit?"

"I have one I've never worn, but I have no intentions of wearing it in front of strangers on this boat."

"It's a ship; bring it along just in case." Sarah figured she could influence Sophie to loosen up once she got there. "Everyone will be too busy worrying about how *they* look in *their* bathing suits to even notice how we look," she added reassuringly.

"Humph."

Later that afternoon the two women left for Hamilton, lists in hand. Sarah drove and Sophie chattered about things people had told her about cruises. She was particularly excited about the casinos onboard. "I didn't know you were a gambler," Sarah teased.

"Not exactly a gambler," Sophie responded, defending her good name. "I just love the excitement." Sarah smiled to herself, knowing that's exactly what gamblers enjoyed about it as well.

Just as Sarah and Sophie arrived at the entrance to the travel agency, another woman walked up to the door. Sarah had just opened the door and she turned to the woman and said, "Go on in," letting her go ahead of them.

"Thank you," the woman said, looking a bit grim.

As they walked toward the counter, the woman stepped back and snapped, "You go first. I'm only ahead of you because you opened the door for me."

Sarah started to argue, but Sophie spoke up saying, "We appreciate that," and she went right up to the counter and said hello to the agent. The woman sat down nearby and picked up a brochure.

Once Sarah explained to the travel agent what they had in mind, the agent got on the computer and pulled up Stephanie Anderson's website. She was able to order Sarah's ticket at the special quilt cruise price and then arranged staterooms for the other two directly with the cruise line.

"We want our rooms to be close together," Sophie interjected.

"I understand," the woman responded. "Do you want two or three rooms?" She looked back and forth between the women, not knowing which one was with Charles.

Before Sophie could speak, Sarah said, "We want three staterooms with balconies, and we want them adjoining."

"Hmm," the woman responded. "That's going to bring you into another price level and ..."

"Not a problem," Sarah said confidently. She enjoyed saying that so much that she added with a sly grin, "... and price is no object." Sophie and the agent looked up simultaneously, first at Sarah and then at each other.

Sophie shrugged. "Give the lady what she wants," she said.

The other woman stood up as Sarah and Sophie completed their transaction. "Excuse me," she said, addressing Sarah. "Did I hear you say you are going on a quilting cruise?"

"Yes," Sarah responded. "I've never done this before, but it sounds like fun. Do you quilt?"

"No, I don't. I wouldn't mind learning though. Could you tell me about it?"

The travel agent, hearing the discussion, said, "I think I have one of Stephanie Anderson's brochures around here somewhere." She fumbled through the papers on her desk and said, "Here it is!" She handed the brochure to the woman and asked if she might be interested.

Turning to Sarah and Sophie, the woman said, "Excuse me. I should have introduced myself. I'm Matilda Knowles. I came in here to buy tickets for a cruise. My husband left it up to me to decide where we would go, and this sounds as if it would be a good choice." Pointing to the brochure she added, "And it looks like they even teach introductory classes." Continuing to read through the brochure, she muttered, "I think I just might do this. This will show the old goat. He can sit in his room and grumble while I have a little fun!"

"There are other activities for spouses and friends," Sarah offered. "Sophie here doesn't quilt and she is going. So is my friend, Charles. Maybe the men can find something to do together."

Matilda frowned, saying, "I don't know. Elwood isn't very sociable."

After saying goodbye to the agent and Matilda, Sophie picked up her cane and the two women left the agency. Suddenly the door behind them flew open and Matilda hurried after them. "Excuse me," she said. "I hope I'm not being too forward, but I was wondering if you would be willing to give me your phone number or email address just in case I get confused about this whole thing. It's all so new to me and I don't know any quilters."

"Of course!" Sarah responded enthusiastically. "In fact, let's meet for lunch and we can make our last minute plans. Do you ever get down to Middletown?"

"It wouldn't be a problem. Is that where you live?"

"Yes, and we have a great quilt shop if you want to buy any of your fabrics."

"Fabrics?" Matilda said hesitantly.

"They provide all the tools, and as soon as you choose your projects, they will send you a list of what fabrics you need to bring. I signed up to buy their kits, so I'm not bringing anything."

"That sounds good. But let's still meet for lunch, okay?"

Sarah suggested they exchange phone numbers and wrote hers down for Matilda. Matilda put it in her purse but said that Elwood napped during the day and didn't like the phone ringing. "I'll call you," she offered.

"We'll see you soon," Sarah called as Matilda headed back into the travel agency to complete her transaction.

Sarah and Sophie headed up the block to Mulligan's Department Store. Originally named Mulligan's Dry Goods, the store had been in business as far back as Sarah could remember. She had shopped at Mulligan's as a teenager and years later had bought many of her children's school clothes there. "It would be sad to lose this store," Sophie said as they walked in. There had been talk of them closing. Mulligan's still used some of their original wooden counters. The aisles were carpeted, but the carpets were well worn and ragged in places.

Looking up, Sophie said, "Remember how there used to be tubes up there like they have now at bank drive-ins? The salesman would put your money in and it would swoop up to the office and your change and receipt would zoom back down?"

"Good grief, Sophie! That was in the 1940s. You have a good memory."

"I have a great memory for the fifties," Sophie said, then added jokingly, "But I barely remember yesterday!"

The women pulled out their lists and made the few purchases they had planned to make; they also made five or six they didn't plan to make. "I have no idea why I suddenly need new underwear just because I'm going on a cruise," Sophie fussed. "And what's wrong with my elephant pajamas?"

They were both tired as they pulled into Sophie's driveway. Sarah gathered up some of Sophie's bags and they headed for her door. Suddenly Sophie was on the ground.

"Sophie!" Sarah screamed, dropping the bags and hurrying to her side. "What happened? Are you hurt?"

"I tripped over the newspaper. I'm okay," Sophie said.

"You tripped over the newspaper?" Sarah asked as she tried to help Sophie up. Unable to get her to her feet, Sarah dialed the Village security office.

"You didn't see it? I don't understand how you could miss it, Sophie. I think you need glasses."

Sophie mumbled something too softly to be heard.

"What did you say?" Sarah asked.

More mumbles.

"Sophie!" Sarah demanded. "What are you saying?"

"I don't need glasses ... I have glasses ..." Sophie sputtered from her position on the sidewalk.

"You have glasses? Why aren't you wearing them? For that matter, why have I never seen them?"

Sophie didn't respond.

"Sophie?" Sarah repeated. "Why aren't you wearing your glasses?"

"Okay," Sophie finally responded. "They make me look like an owl."

Sarah sighed and shook her head. Just then, the security officer picked up the phone. "How can I help you?" he asked.

"I have a friend lying on the ground. She can't get up and I can't lift her. Can you send someone?"

"How did she end up on the ground?" the officer asked after confirming their exact location.

"She doesn't want to look like an owl," Sarah responded.

"I beg your pardon?" the officer said, assuming he had misunderstood.

Sarah sighed again and said, "Never mind. Just send us a strong man or two." She hung up and sat down on the curb with Sophie, awaiting help.

"I'm sorry," a very small voice said from the sidewalk.

Paul from the security office got Sophie into the house and confirmed that nothing was broken, although Sarah was concerned about her ankle. Sophie assured her it didn't hurt at all. The only injury seemed to be a scraped hand where she caught herself going down.

"Tomorrow we are taking your glasses back and getting you a pair you like, okay?"

"Okay," Sophie responded, her voice still very small.

Sarah was pleased to know that the question of why Sophie was falling had finally been answered.

* * * * *

The next three weeks were very busy ones for Sarah and Sophie as they excitedly prepared for the trip. One afternoon Sarah was in Sophie's bedroom helping her decide which clothes to take and which to leave at home. At the moment, she had about five suitcases worth of clothes piled on her bed.

"Do I need to buy a life jacket?" Sophie asked as she started hanging up some of the things Sarah had told her she wouldn't need.

"Of course not, Sophie! They will have plenty of life jackets on the ship."

"But how do I know they'll fit?"

"They'll fit, Sophie. They fit everyone."

"Will they come in extra-wide *petite*? If not, they won't fit me right."

"Sophie! Relax! You aren't going to need a life jacket, but if you do, they will fit you. I promise!"

"Just remember I can't swim," she muttered as she continued hanging clothes back in the closet.

"And how about Barney?" Sophie asked nervously. Sophie hadn't done much traveling, and the idea of going so far from home had her a bit edgy.

"Caitlyn and Andy are going to take care of him. He's going to their house the day before we leave since we will be heading for the airport early."

Sarah and Caitlyn had been meeting several afternoons each week and most of the blocks for her father's quilt were made. Caitlyn seemed to have a real knack for sewing. She was accurate with her seam allowances and was very careful to cut precisely. Sarah taught her how to square up her blocks, but in most cases they were coming out exactly right without trimming. They still had two months until Andy's birthday, which was plenty of time to finish and get the quilt top to Kimberly for quilting.

"I'm glad we are going to fly. That'll make the trip go faster," Sophie responded. Once Sarah had deposited the check from her aunt Rose, she had realized it would make more sense to buy three airline tickets and fly to Baltimore. She hadn't even asked the other two for their opinions; she just did it. Charles had been looking forward to the train trip, but she promised him they would take a scenic train trip later on and that the object right now was to get to Baltimore.

One afternoon, Sarah and Sophie met Matilda for lunch at the café across the street from Stitches. Matilda explained that she was all signed up and ready to go. She had spoken with one of the instructors, who helped her pick her classes. Matilda had never used a sewing machine, so she decided to choose only the classes where she could sew by hand. The instructor promised to give her personal help in learning the few stitches she would need in order to do both piecing and appliqué. The only other time Sarah had seen Matilda she had seemed very aloof and cold, but as they talked at lunch she could see that Matilda was probably just uncomfortable around strangers. "She is certainly excited about the classes," Sarah said later to Sophie.

"I'm surprised she is bringing her husband along, though," Sophie responded. "She doesn't seem to like him much."

Sarah laughed. "I don't know if that's it. But they do seem to be having some problems getting along right now. She said he wasn't pleased about the quilting aspect of the trip, but she didn't seem to particularly care what he thought about it." Sarah became very quiet, obviously thinking about what she had just said.

"Don't worry! You and lover boy will never have that problem. You two are like a couple of playful kittens together!" Sophie said with a cackle.

"I hope you're right," Sarah responded, much too seriously for Sophie.

"Lighten up, kid."

Chapter 12

Bleep ... bleep ... bleep ... bleep ... bleep ... bleep ... bleep ... bleep ...

The voice of the Captain blared over the loud speaker as he attempted to be heard over the sound of the ship's emergency sirens.

"There is no emergency, folks. Please remain calm. The alarm was set off by accident. Will the passengers who left the ship please return? If you have already checked in with the purser, just continue through to your stateroom."

There was general chaos as the purser attempted to determine who had been checked in and who had not.

"I'm Matilda Knowles. Have you seen my husband?" The woman appeared frantic as she attempted to get the purser's attention through the crowd.

"I'm sorry, Mrs. Knowles," the purser called. "Everything is chaotic right now, and I don't have any idea who is here and not here." Looking at his roster, he called to her as she was walking away, "Wait, Mrs. Knowles. I see his name on the list. He checked in about an hour ago. I'll check you in now. You two are in 8010 on the Mercury Deck. Turn right at the atrium and take the elevator to the eighth deck."

"Thank you," Matilda called over her shoulder as she headed inside.

The purser turned to his assistant and said, "I'm sure glad this trip doesn't require passports. We would have to empty the ship and start over. I have no idea who has boarded and who hasn't!"

"Come on, Sophie. Charles already checked us in. We can head on up to our staterooms."

Sarah turned away from Sophie so she wouldn't see her smile as Sophie slipped on her new glasses. The very large, very round purple frames were embedded with sparkling stones mimicking diamonds. Sophie held her head high, proudly displaying her purchase. Sarah wondered what Matilda had thought when the two women walked into the café the previous week with Sophie sporting her new glasses and hot-pink cruise outfit.

"We're in 3001, 3, and 5." As they took the elevator up, Sarah pointed out the deck diagram. Each floor was named after a planet in the solar system going toward the sun, which was, of course, the top deck.

"I see most of the shops are on the Earth deck," Sophie noted. "Earth people love their shopping!"

Their staterooms were on the Saturn deck, the third of the nine decks available to passengers. They were each carrying overnight bags as they were instructed since there was no guarantee when their luggage would arrive. As they approached their staterooms, however, they saw all three doors standing open and their luggage already inside. Charles appeared from his room smiling. "Go on in, ladies. Your rooms await." Turning to Sarah he said, "I wasn't expecting anything like this! I'd been warned to expect closets for rooms, but these rooms are a nice size."

"They have rooms that are much smaller," Sarah responded. "We went for the larger ones," she added, looking proud of her extravagance.

Sarah and Sophie went into Sophie's room first and then hurried over to Sarah's. They were identical except for the colors. Sophie's had been decorated in autumn colors and Sarah's was in shades of blue. They were bright and roomy, each with a large patio-type sliding glass door that opened onto a small balcony. A queen-size bed ran parallel to the balcony door so one could lie in bed and watch the sea go by.

Just inside the room, there was a love seat on the left wall facing a small table with two bucket chairs on the right. Above the table was a wall-mounted television screen. On each side of the room there was a locked door, which Charles explained opened into the adjoining staterooms. He unlocked the door on the left wall and led Sophie back into her room.

"This is perfect!" Sarah exclaimed, walking around the foot of her bed and standing at the balcony door. Charles walked over and stood beside her. "This is going to be a great adventure," Sarah said, looking up at him with a smile. Charles winked and squeezed her hand.

After a few quiet moments, Charles gave Sarah a kiss on her cheek and said, "I'm going to go unpack." Charles didn't open their adjoining door but went into the corridor and on to his own room next door.

On an upper deck, Matilda was also unpacking. She hung her clothes on the right side of the built-in wardrobe and Elwood's on the left. She then put all of their folded items, socks, underwear, and the like into the built-in drawers. The room was spacious and included a sitting room alcove. Looking out at the private balcony, she was glad she had decided on a penthouse suite. There were two beds that could be put together to form a California king. She would keep them separate. Matilda opened the French doors and walked out onto the balcony. There was a soft breeze that played with the curls around her face. She was eager to feel the ship pulling out of the dock. They had been planning this trip for over a year, working out all the details. She thought about the insurance money and smiled. *This could be a very profitable trip*, she thought.

Matilda Knowles caught a glimpse of herself in the bathroom mirror as she was placing their personal items on the shelf. She looked tired and drawn. She dabbed on some lipstick and ran her fingers over her short brown hair, rearranging the curls. Matilda Knowles was a tall woman, tall and thin. At sixty-four years old, she was beginning to show her age. She vowed to eat more on the cruise and perhaps fill out a bit.

It was late afternoon before everyone had finally boarded. The ship would be leaving the dock soon and travelling south for several days on their way to San Juan and the U.S. Virgin Islands. Matilda was tired and decided to sit on the balcony for a while and maybe even take a nap before dinner.

* * * * *

The steward led Elwood Knowles to a round table, which appeared to be set for eight guests. "Will your wife be joining you?" he asked as Knowles took a seat on the far side of the table facing the entrance.

"I don't think so," he responded. "She is tired from the flight. She might eat later."

"You can get food anytime in the café on the Mars deck," he responded and took Knowles' drink order. He ordered a dry martini with two olives. As he was sipping his drink, the steward brought another couple to the table and pulled out two chairs. He introduced them to Knowles as "Ms. Sarah Miller and Mr. Charles Parker."

"Good evening, Mr. Knowles. Nice to meet you," Sarah said politely. "Are you alone?"

"My wife may join us. She wanted a short nap."

"I wouldn't mind a nap myself," Charles said with a chuckle, reaching his arm across the table to offer a firm handshake. "Glad to meet you, Knowles," he said. Turning toward Sarah, he added, "Is Sophie planning to join us?"

"She said she is going to skip dinner, but knowing Sophie, she will be starved in an hour or two. I think I'll order a meal to take to her if she doesn't get here before we finish."

"Just let your cabin steward know what you want," the wine steward said as he stopped at the table to get their drink orders. "He'll bring it to the room."

"Thank you," Sarah said with a smile.

After they had placed their orders, Charles studied Mr. Knowles as only an ex-cop can. Knowles appeared to be in his mid-sixties with gray hair and a sallow complexion. There was a middle-aged man Charles had met some years earlier when he was investigating a crime in the Theater District. He didn't know why the memory of that man came to him at this moment, except that Mr. Knowles had that same effeminate look.

"What's your line, Knowles?" he asked, although he was sure this wasn't the same man.

"Oh, this and that. Actually not much of anything right now. How about you?" Knowles asked, effectively taking the focus off of himself.

"Retired cop," Charles answered confidently. Elwood Knowles didn't respond, but picked up the menu and put his glasses on. When the steward returned with the drinks, Knowles lifted his glass, gesturing for a refill without looking at Charles.

Two more couples joined them, and introductions went around the table. Dinner conversation was light and inconsequential. "Is this your first cruise?" the new addition to the table asked, looking directly at Sarah.

"Actually, it is. I probably wouldn't be here except for the quilting classes. That sounded intriguing to me. Do you quilt?"

"Oh, no," the woman responded as if she were proudly protecting her non-quilter status. "We cruise every year. It's our first time on this ship. Where are you quilting people going to be working?" she asked, sounding as if she wanted to avoid that area.

"Tomorrow we meet in the auditorium on the Jupiter deck. After that, I don't know yet," Sarah responded with a patient smile.

The group ordered dinner and continued light conversation. Elwood Knowles stayed to himself, speaking only when he was directly addressed. After eating, Charles and Sarah excused themselves and went out on the deck. It was windy, but it felt refreshing to both of them.

They stopped at the railing and looked at the moon reflected on the water. He was holding her hand. He raised it to his lips and gently kissed her palm. She nestled closer to him, and they stayed like that for a long time, watching the lights along the shoreline in the far distance as the ship cut a path through the darkness.

Chapter 13

"Welcome to our ninth annual quilting cruise!" The woman at the front of the room seemed like an old friend. Sarah had purchased one of her instruction tapes and studied it diligently. Stephanie Anderson was well known in quilting circles for her meticulous appliqué and piecing. She was a sought-after instructor, and Sarah felt fortunate to have this opportunity to learn from her.

The speaker continued, "I'm here with three other instructors, and we have an exciting program planned for our time together. First of all, I'm Stephanie Anderson—please call me Stephanie. This is Mary Kate, Delores, and Lillian. You have name tags in your packets, and we hope you'll wear them. We're all going to make many new friends."

Stephanie went on to talk about the cruise. "As you all know, this is an eleven-day cruise, counting the day we boarded and the day we return. We'll have three days at sea as we follow the coastline south, and we have classes scheduled on all those days. We will arrive in Puerto Rico on the fifth day. You'll have two days there to explore. Then we'll move on to St. Thomas for a day to enjoy the island beaches."

"Are there fabric shops in San Juan?" one of the participants asked, and everyone laughed.

"They aren't the quilting shops you are accustomed to, but you can talk to the purser about shopping and learn all about the land excursions. I've been told you should also watch for fabrics sold by the street vendors. Again, they may not be the cottons we're used to, but they are certainly worth taking a look at."

"What if we don't go on the excursions? Can we sew?" someone in the audience asked.

"Absolutely! We'll have instructors here all day every day, and the sewing areas will be available all night long for the night owls!" Continuing with her overview of the cruise, Stephanie said, "So that's three days at sea with classes offered every day, three days on the islands, and three more days at sea on our return, with classes and workshops every day. We will arrive back in our homeport on the eleventh day. Any questions?"

Since there were no questions, Stephanie continued. "Now, let's talk about the classes." Before the cruise, everyone had received descriptions of the classes, pictures of the finished projects, and a registration form so they could preregister. Kits could be ordered at that time, or participants could bring their own fabrics.

"I wanted to let you know that if you change your mind about any of the classes you signed up for—or if you want to change your choices or add a class or two—just see me, and I'll help you rearrange your schedule. This is *your* time!"

One of the participants toward the back stood to ask a question. "I was already thinking I wanted to change my class, but I brought materials for the one I signed up for. What if it isn't right?"

"Good question," Stephanie responded. "I have several boxes of fat quarters that you can purchase, and they'll work for most of our projects. I'll be happy to help you with that."

"Thank you," the woman responded, sitting back down.

Sarah had chosen an appliqué class that was being taught by Stephanie. She would be making a small wallhanging with a pieced background and an appliquéd foreground, and she was excited about learning this new skill from an expert. She planned to put it in her living room. Sarah also signed up for the machine quilting class taught by one of the other instructors, as well as the paper-piecing class.

Sarah found it hard to believe there would be time for all the projects. She was going to make the tote bag, and the class description said it could be made in a few hours. She was tentatively signed up to make a throw but wasn't sure there would be time. She would be very busy with the classes she had.

Looking at the samples of all the projects, Sarah was glad she had ordered the kits. The colors were spectacular and not at all what she would have chosen. She was glad that she was going to be stretched beyond her comfort zone.

Stephanie went on to describe the various classes and where they would meet. For this introductory meeting, the group was using the auditorium at one end of the Jupiter deck. A portion of the deck directly adjacent to the auditorium was set aside for classes. Dividers had been used to form classrooms that were outfitted with individual workstations.

Stephanie continued, "Beyond the classrooms, you will find a large area marked *Workroom*. There are extra sewing machines in that area, and you can come use them anytime you want. This whole area will be open around the clock, so if you are a night owl, come on in and make yourself at home! Now, are there any other questions?"

A hand popped up in the third row. "Will we be having a show-and-tell?"

"Absolutely!" Stephanie replied. "Have you ever known a quilting group that didn't want to show off their work?" The group laughed their agreement. "We'll do that right here in the auditorium on one of the last days. Any other questions?" The group was silent.

It was a warm sunny day, and Sarah's eyes kept wandering toward the balcony doors. Just then Stephanie said, "And I know you are all eager to get familiar with the ship and all its amenities. Our first classes are scheduled for this afternoon starting at 1:00. Enjoy the next few hours at sea. Explore and have fun!"

Sarah hadn't signed up for any classes until the next day so that she and Charles could have some time together. She also wanted to make sure Sophie was settled into the ship before she was gone all day in classes. As she was leaving the auditorium, she spotted Matilda sitting in a back row. She maneuvered her way over to where she was sitting, smiling as she approached. At first Matilda looked at her as if she didn't recognize her, but suddenly she smiled. "Sorry," she said. "I was a million miles away."

"I could tell you were deep in thought. Is it anything you want to share?"

"I was just watching the other participants and noticing the wide range of ages. I was surprised to see so many young women involved in quilting." Actually, her thoughts had gone far beyond that. She had wondered what it would have been like to grow up with a mother who had taught her to sew, cook, or do any of the things she imagined mothers and daughters did together. Instead, Matilda had remained in an orphanage until she was sixteen and had learned to fight her way through life. When she was eighteen, she had married a petty thief who beat her daily. Fortunately, he ended up in prison. She swore she would be more careful in the future. When she met Elwood, she knew he would never hurt her—at least not physically. He appeared to be weak and easy to manipulate. Despite being quiet and reserved, he had a pathological desire to be near strong women, and marriage didn't change that. He continued to seek out other strong women after they were married.

Sarah looked around and smiled. "You're right! Quilting is becoming very popular. When is your first class?"

"This afternoon. I'm signed up for Piecing by Hand. It's a beginner's class."

"Is that today?" Sarah said rhetorically, wishing she had signed up for it.

"Yes, it starts at two this afternoon. They are going to offer it again in a few days."

"Sophie doesn't quilt, but I would love for her to learn. She doesn't seem to have any interest. In fact, I could barely talk her into coming on the cruise since it was billed as a *quilting* cruise. I think she would enjoy it if she would just give it a try."

The woman smiled and nodded knowingly. "My husband thought I was crazy!" Pulling out the instructions she had received about the introductory class, she handed it to Sarah and said, "You can show her this. I think she could probably get in the class. Why don't you ask Stephanie? She's walking this way."

Sarah waved to Stephanie, indicating that she had a question. After stopping to speak to several other people, Stephanie joined the two women. After exchanging introductions, she confirmed that the beginning classes would be open to anyone on the cruise. "We always encourage new quilters to give it a try." Stephanie explained that they were going to let the new folks decide whether they wanted to learn machine or hand piecing.

"Hand piecing would be perfect for my friend. She claims she doesn't believe in technology," Sarah said with a chuckle. "Actually, I wouldn't mind having some instruction on hand piecing myself if there's time."

During the two hours she had spent hand piecing with Grace, she realized she had really enjoyed it. It felt more peaceful than machine piecing. For a moment she pictured herself and Sophie sitting across from each other on Sophie's porch, hand piecing and chatting.

But then reality set in, and she had to stifle a laugh.

* * * * *

"Quilting? Now, you know better," Sophie said frowning playfully. "Can you just imagine me sitting in my rocking chair with a cat at my feet, playing with a ball of yarn?"

"There's no yarn involved in quilting, Sophie. Come on. It'll be fun! You won't have to use a sewing machine. We'll learn how to piece the fabric by hand, and we'll do it together. Okay?" Sarah pleaded.

"Humph."

About that time, Charles came up to the two women where they were stretched out on deck chairs enjoying the warm sunshine. "How about a little lunch?" He explained that he wanted to take them up to the Mars deck, where he had found an outdoor café that served salads and sandwiches. Secretly, he also wanted to show Sarah the pool, hoping she would go swimming with him later.

"Perfect! Saved by the bell," Sophie responded, struggling to get up from the deck chair.

Charles gave her a hand and asked, "Saved from what?"

"Your girlfriend is trying to recruit me into that quilting cult she is mixed up with. Let's eat."

Shaking her head, Sarah fell in line behind Sophie, and the three headed for the café. As they were being seated, Sarah spotted Matilda coming in alone. "Matilda," she called out. "Would you like to join us?" Matilda looked unsure but walked over to their table. Charles stood as she approached, and Sarah smiled at his gallantry.

"I don't know," Matilda began. "I'm not sure if my husband is going to get here. He wanted to talk to the captain about making a ship-to-shore call. Our cell phones aren't working out here."

"Well, we'd love to have you join us. This is my friend, Charles Parker, and you already know Sophie Ward." Turning to Charles, she said, "And this is Matilda Knowles. We met at the travel office, and she is in the quilting classes."

Charles shook her hand and pulled out a chair for her. "You're from Middletown, too?" he asked.

"No, we live just outside Hamilton," she offered briefly.

"Hi, Matilda. You were talking about me?" Sophie said looking unduly suspicious. "And just what were you two saying about me?"

Sarah spoke up, answering Sophie's question. "I was telling Matilda how excited you would be to learn that there was an opening in the beginners class!" Matilda looked a bit puzzled since that was not at all the gist of their conversation. "Humph."

When the waitress came to take their orders, Matilda didn't seem to know what to do.

"Does he know you're in this café?" Sarah asked.

"Yes. He said he would try to meet me here once he took care of his business. He's always working!"

"Why don't we watch for him? In the meantime, let's have some lunch," Sophie suggested, eager to have the food served.

"Knowles," Charles repeated. "Knowles. We met a Knowles last night at dinner. I don't think I caught his first name ..."

"Elwood," Matilda offered. "Elwood's my husband's name."

"Your husband is Elwood Knowles?" Sarah said in amazement. "We had dinner with him last night, and I had no idea he was your husband. I don't know why I didn't make the connection."

"So!" Charles exclaimed. "Your husband is Elwood Knowles. That's interesting." *The wife says he's "always working," and he told us he didn't do much of anything.*

Matilda looked surprised. "Why is that interesting?" But before he could answer, Matilda realized her mistake. *I've got to be more careful,* she thought.

"I guess it's not exactly *interesting*," Charles corrected. "It's just that we sat at his table last night ..."

"Excuse my friend," Sarah interrupted apologetically. "He is always analyzing. Now let's order. This poor woman has been standing here all this time waiting for us to order."

"Oh," Charles said looking embarrassed. "Sorry, Miss."

The table of four ordered ice tea all around, gazpacho, and an assortment of finger sandwiches. "I want to eat light," Charles said, "because I'm looking forward to swimming some laps this afternoon."

He winked at Sarah and again marveled at what an attractive woman she was. *And always has been*, he thought. Her long blond hair of twenty years earlier was now cropped just below her ears and was various degrees of curly depending on the weather. There were gray streaks around her temples, but she didn't do anything to conceal them. She was trim and dressed casually but always looked feminine. Her eyes were as blue as the sea and her skin surprisingly soft and smooth for a sixty-nine-year-old woman. *Or am I just biased?* he wondered.

There was no question in his mind that he was in love with this gentle woman. She, on the other hand, seemed to be struggling with her feelings for him. He hoped they could talk about it one day, but not on this trip. This trip was special. Hopefully it was a chance for them to get to know one another at a deeper level.

"Where have you gone?" Sarah asked, placing her hand on his arm. He rested his hand on top of hers and patted it gently. He smiled and she blushed ever so slightly, as if she knew he had been thinking about her.

Sophie looked beyond the railing at the panoramic view of the ocean and said, "Are you allowed to do that?"

"Allowed to do what?" Charles asked, forgetting his original statement.

"Swim laps," she said, again looking out at the sea. Her tone was so serious that no one realized she was kidding, and Charles began to explain about the pool.

"Stop!" Sophie said, holding her hand up like a crossing guard. "I know. I saw the pool. And ..." she added, turning to Matilda, "... I have no intention of picking up a needle and thread."

Chapter 14

After lunch, the three friends returned to their staterooms and Matilda headed for her penthouse suite on the Mercury deck. Elwood missed lunch, but Matilda had ordered a sandwich to be delivered to their suite. "He gets really obnoxious when he misses a meal," Matilda had explained. "I think it's his blood sugar, but he doesn't believe in doctors." Although her words suggested concern for her husband, Charles noticed a sharpness in her voice that belied that concern. Her eyes darkened and were cold when she talked about him. Sometimes he wished he didn't notice all the nuances.

Charles and Sarah discussed going to the pool, but Sarah was feeling tired from all the excitement and wanted to take it easy for a few hours. She and Sophie decided to take the elevator up to the top deck. Once they arrived on the Sun deck, they found a line of deck chairs. They rubbed on sunscreen and stretch out on adjoining deck chairs.

The sun was warm on Sarah's face, and occasionally she imagined that she felt a light spray from the ocean. Sea gulls were swooping down toward the deck, checking for stray bits of food. Now and then, one would light on the railing and stare at her as if to say, "Feed me!"

Barney gives me that same look, Sarah thought. She missed him. *How silly to miss my dog!* But Barney was the love of her life with his shaggy brown coat and forlorn eyes. Thinking about Barney brought a smile to her face.

"What's that silly smile about?" Sophie asked. "Are you thinking about that cute fella of yours?"

"I'm thinking about a cute fella alright, but not the one you're suggesting," Sarah responded.

"Oh?" Sophie said, removing the towel from her face and rising up in the deck chair to look at Sarah. "And who, then?"

"My adorable dog, Barney."

"Oh no! Not that straggly looking mutt! I don't know what you see in him." Sophie added, lying back down on her chair.

Sophie had pretended to dislike Barney from the beginning, but Sarah knew they had a very special bond. When Sophie thought she wasn't looking, Sarah would catch a tender moment passing between them. "Is someone going to go in and feed him while you're away?" Sophie asked.

"Sophie! You know I didn't leave him alone for nearly two weeks! He has moved up the street with Andy and Caitlyn. Caitlyn loves him, and he never looked back when I left him there," she added almost sadly.

"How is Andy doing?"

"He's doing fine. That computer class he was teaching at the prison has become a part-time job for him. And he and Caitlyn are having a great time getting to know each other.

Andy is doing everything he can to make up for the years they missed together."

"What has happened with the Village management people? Are they still giving him grief about having someone under fifty-five living there?" Sophie asked.

"Andy went to an attorney who found a loophole allowing her to stay, thank goodness. Caitlyn is now his official live-in caregiver!" Sarah said with a smile.

About that time, a man walked up and said, "Is this chair taken?"

Sophie sarcastically responded, "No, it's still here. Are you planning to take it?"

The man smiled, stretched out full length on the deck chair, and sighed deeply. "Ah, this is the life!" Sitting back up, he turned to Sophie and said, "My name is Worme, Jeffrey Worme."

"Worm?" Sophie repeated.

"Yes, but it's spelled with an *e* on the end: *w-o-r-m-e*."

"That's unusual," Sarah interjected. "Where are you from?"

"I'm from right here."

"Right *here*?" Sophie asked, pointing down at the deck.

"Well, not right here. I mean here in the United States. But my parents were from Germany. They came to this country before I was born. My father used to say we got our name from the ancient city of Worms in southern Germany, but …"

"More than I need to know," Sophie interrupted, covering her face with a towel. Jeffrey Worme lay back down and smiled. *Feisty lady*, he thought.

Jeffrey was short with a broad build, not exactly overweight but sturdy. His hair was black and perhaps just a little *too* black, Sophie noted. "I don't trust a man who dyes his hair," she said to Sarah when they returned to their room. He had tried several times to strike up a conversation with Sophie, but she nipped every attempt in the bud.

"I think he likes you," Sarah said teasingly.

"Well, he's wasting his time if that's the case," Sophie responded as she prepared to take a shower. "I'm going to an early dinner tonight. You and *lover boy* can find a romantic spot to dine under the stars."

Later that afternoon, as Sophie walked toward an informal café, Jeffrey Worme appeared at her side. "Would you be willing to stop in the Beach Bum Lounge with me for a drink before you have dinner?" he asked cautiously, knowing this fascinating woman was capable of cutting him down with a look.

"Yes. That would be lovely," Sophie responded, in a sweet tone that caught Jeffrey totally off guard.

"It would?" he asked, a bit confused.

"Did you want me to say no?" she demanded, frowning.

"No! Absolutely not! I was hoping you would say yes. It just surprised me when you did," he responded with a smile. He reached to take her arm, but she yanked it away from him. Together they entered the bar, and he led her to a table in the corner. "Let's sit over here so we can talk."

"Humph."

Jeffrey had to work very hard to get Sophie engaged in a conversation, but once she started, they actually had a good time. Sophie had a contagious laugh that he enjoyed, as well as a huge repertoire of stories about life in Cunningham

Village. His favorite story was about the hula hoop class she took the previous year. He could just picture this short chubby woman attempting to keep a hoop twirling. In her version of the class, she had been the star. She would not, however, be telling this version in front of Sarah, who knew better.

After a couple of drinks, Sophie agreed to have dinner with him, but she declared she wasn't in the mood for a fancy restaurant. They walked around the ship, looking at the many eating establishments available to them, and settled on a simple outdoor buffet. After dinner they strolled along the deck, talking and laughing. Sophie had left her cane in the room and had to hold onto Jeffrey's arm as they walked. She would never admit it, even to herself, but she enjoyed the closeness.

Sophie's husband had been gone for many years. He died in the nursing home just a few years earlier, but she had lost him many years before that as she watched him fade into Alzheimer's. The last year he didn't know her, and it became harder and harder to visit him. "Where have you gone?" Jeffrey asked gently, realizing she was deep in thought.

"Oh, just enjoying the warm breeze," she responded. It was just dusk, and they found themselves back at the Beach Bum Lounge.

"Would you like a dessert drink?" he asked.

"No—I would like a real dessert!" she responded, pointing toward a fifties-style ice-cream shop. After their bowls were filled with ice cream, the steward offered a delectable array of toppings. Sophie chose fresh strawberries, nuts, hot fudge, and a whopping glob of whipped cream that crept over the edge of her bowl. "Yum!" she exclaimed with a mischievous grin as she cleaned it off the bowl and licked her finger.

Later, Jeffrey walked Sophie back to her stateroom. "Would you like to do something tomorrow?"

"Like what?" she asked suspiciously.

"I don't know. Why don't you take a look at the ship's cable channel? It tells you about all the activities on the ship. You pick one. I'm game for anything," he responded.

"I'll bet you are," she responded acidly and went into the stateroom, closing the door behind her. Jeffrey remained outside her door for a few moments, thinking about this feisty lady. Sophie remained inside the door for a few moments, smiling.

Chapter 15

After an exciting evening with Charles, followed by a good night's sleep, Sarah entered the quilting area eager for her first class. Thinking back over the evening, she was glad she had decided to bring two cocktail dresses. The floor show was in one of the elegant dinner clubs, and she was able to dress up and still have another dress for the formal dinner. Charles seemed to have been taken aback when she opened the stateroom door dressed in a sleek black dress and matching heels. He was accustomed to seeing her in casual clothes and was overwhelmed. "You're dazzling," he had said.

Sarah pulled the schedule out of her packet and headed for Classroom B. There were already several women at workstations. She chose a table close to the front of the room, assuming that was where Stephanie would be standing. She opened her kit and spread out the vibrant colored batiks in shades of blue and green with yellow, orange, and gold highlights swirling randomly throughout. Meanwhile, another five or six women took seats around the room.

Stephanie had already pinned a sample wallhanging to the front wall. Looking at it closely, Sarah could see that the background was pieced with varying shades of neutral batiks. On this background, Stephanie had appliquéd a vase of gracefully arranged flowers, one flower actually extending beyond the background and onto the outer border. It was this detail that had caused Sarah to choose this particular project. She loved the concept of things refusing to remain inside their assigned boundaries.

"Hi, folks," Stephanie announced, beaming as she walked into the room. "It looks like everyone is here." She started the class right away after introductions. The first step was to make the simple background for their wallhanging. Stephanie passed out instruction sheets and encouraged people to read the whole sheet before starting. They then cut the squares, rearranged them until they were happy with the placement, and sewed them together to form a background piece about twelve inches square. They then added a one-inch inner border and a three-inch outer border. As each student completed this base, they were ready to meet with Stephanie individually to learn how to cut and apply the vase and flowers.

Sarah was pleased with her background and borders. She caught on quickly to the needle-turn appliqué technique Stephanie was teaching. Sarah smiled to herself as she stitched.

The class broke for lunch, and Sarah excitedly rushed back to the stateroom to show Sophie and Charles her handiwork. Both rooms were empty, so she freshened up and headed for what had become their favorite place to sit and watch the coastline in the far distance. Just as she suspected, Sophie and Charles were stretched out on deck chairs, both covered with towels. The sun was very strong that day but felt delightful as Sarah joined her friends. "How about some lunch?" she suggested as she sat down.

"Well hello there, pretty lady," Charles said as he sat up. "How much time do we have with you?"

"The class doesn't resume for two hours, but we're working on our own until we finish the handwork so it doesn't matter when I get back. What did you have in mind?" she asked in a coy tone. He raised an eyebrow and she blushed. They both laughed a bit self-consciously.

"Humph," Sophie responded, without removing the towel from her face.

"Sorry," he said. "I was just hoping for a dip in the pool before lunch."

"Let's do it!" Sarah said enthusiastically.

"Not me!" Sophie interjected, removing the towel from her face. "I'm hungry."

"Then I got here just in time!" Jeffrey was just walking up from a lower deck with a big grin on his face. His coal black hair glistened in the sunlight. "Shall we go get some lunch, fair lady?" he said to Sophie as he joined the group. "Hi, folks," he added, addressing Sarah and Charles. He extended his hand to Charles, saying, "I'm Jeffrey Worme."

"Charles Parker," Charles responded. They stood and chatted for a few minutes and then separated to head in their respective directions. Charles and Sarah strolled toward their rooms to change into their bathing suits, and Sophie and Jeffrey headed for one of the many cafés. "What's with that hair?" Charles asked Sarah, and they both chuckled.

Later, as they approached the top deck, Sarah looked again in awe at the huge slide that swirled its way from high above the deck down to the pool. The first time she saw it, she assured herself she wouldn't go near it. "Are you up for it?" Charles asked.

Sarah hesitated. At sixty-nine, she was way beyond the age of craving this degree of excitement; on the other hand, she knew it would be an exhilarating experience. "Are you going up?" she asked Charles.

"I will if you will," was his not-so-helpful response.

"Oh, what the heck. Let's just do it!" Sarah announced, walking quickly toward the ladder and hoping to get there before she changed her mind. As she climbed to the top, she could feel her whole body trembling. *What am I doing?* she asked herself. She sat down on the launching pad and peered down, but she couldn't see the water because of the wide curves in the slide. For a moment, she considered turning around and climbing back down the ladder. Charles was right behind her and tenderly laid his hand on her shoulder.

"Do you want to climb back down?" he asked gently.

"I'll take this route down," she responded, pointing her toes down the slide before she could change her mind. Sarah pushed herself off and screamed all the way down as she whirled through the slippery curves. With a huge splash, she was in the water and struggling to get acclimated. She felt her body naturally heading for the surface and, once there, she swam to the side of the pool to watch for Charles (who, as it turned out, was right behind her).

"Shall we go again?" Charles asked as they got out of the pool. He was shaking his head vigorously to clear the water from his hair.

"Did you learn that move from Barney?" she asked while reaching for a towel to dry her face. "And to answer your question, that was an incredible experience that I will never forget and will never repeat!"

After adapting to relatively solid ground, the two got into the lap pool and leisurely swam back and forth until they tired.

Sarah decided to skip lunch so she wouldn't be late for the afternoon session, and Charles ordered lunch to be delivered to his room. "See you later, sweetie," Charles said, kissing her cheek as she headed for her room to change. The afternoon session was spent working on their projects. Stephanie demonstrated how to do inward and outward curves and points. Sarah was surprised how quickly her wallhanging was taking shape. It occurred to her that she might be able to quilt it herself once she learned how to machine quilt. She was hoping she wouldn't be returning home with a bunch of unfinished projects.

Because Sarah didn't need instructions at this point, she moved to the workshop where the doors to the deck were open and where she could feel the soft ocean breeze. Her mind wandered to thoughts of Charles and their relationship. Despite her original misgivings, they had become very close. She enjoyed his attention and the way he so often anticipated her needs even before she did. She was glad she had invited him on the cruise. She had been reluctant at first, but Sophie convinced her it would be a chance for them to get to know each other better. "You can't learn much about a person hanging around an old folks' home," Sophie had said. Sarah was tired of telling her it was *not* an old folks' home, so she just let it go.

Sarah knew why she had been hesitant to invite Charles, but she hadn't told Sophie. The fact was that she was worried about their sleeping arrangements. She and Charles had never discussed moving their relationship beyond where it has been for two years. They were the closest of friends and were very affectionate with one another. They clearly loved each other, but she still struggled with the idea of becoming intimate with another man. Jonathan had been her husband and lover since she graduated from high school. She just couldn't shake the feeling that she would be disloyal to him. He had been gone for over twenty years, and she knew that was irrational thinking. Knowing, however, was sometimes not enough.

Sarah continued to stitch until after five, when Stephanie came by to say goodbye to the four or five women who had joined Sarah in the workshop. Stephanie explained she would be available in the classroom the next morning if anyone had problems or questions, but she wasn't scheduled to teach until the afternoon.

"What are you signed up for tomorrow, Sarah?" Stephanie asked.

"I'm spending the afternoon in Delores' machine quilting class. Once I get my appliqué finished, I hope to quilt it by machine before I go home."

"That's an ambitious plan," Stephanie said simply. "Your appliqué work is beautiful by the way," she added as she walked away.

An hour later, Sarah slipped her project into her quilting tote and headed to her room, still smiling from the pleasure of receiving a compliment from a much-respected quilter.

Chapter 16

Having skipped lunch, Sarah was hungry, so she and Charles headed out for an early dinner. Charles suggested they check out the Venus deck with its collection of small restaurants offering cuisine from around the world. The couple walked slowly through the area, reading menus and talking to staff that were stationed outside the restaurants to answer questions and offer samples. The doorways to the restaurants were almost as wide as the restaurants themselves, giving an easy view of the inside. Sarah stopped at an Ethiopian restaurant and accepted a sample, not having any idea what the food was like. The waiter, dressed in native garb, offered her a taste of what he called *doro wat* in a small piece of pita. He explained it was chicken cooked with onions and spiced butter.

"Zesty," she said, waving her hand in front of her mouth to indicate the level of spicy heat.

They moved on past several restaurants serving European, French, German, Italian, and Greek cuisine. "We can get these in Hamilton," Charles noted. "Let's pick something totally different."

They paused at a Cuban restaurant, and this time Charles accepted a sample. Sarah refused the waiter's offer, still recovering from the Ethiopian spices. The waiter offered Charles a rather large helping of *picadillo a lo nene*, explaining that it was made with ground beef, olives, capers, potatoes, onions, and green peppers. He was very impressed but was still curious about what else was available.

Moving on, they came to the Asian restaurants. He walked ahead but noticed Sarah had stopped to speak with the waiter outside the Burmese restaurant. As Charles approached, he heard the man explaining that Burmese cuisine was a blend of foods from India, China, and Thailand. "That sounds fascinating," Sarah was saying. She accepted a sample and nodded her head approvingly.

"Is this it?" Charles asked. They looked in at the low tables and patrons sitting on mats on the floor.

"Let's do it," she said with an eager smile, hoping she could get back up gracefully and without help.

The couple lingered for two hours over their meal, talking about the cruise, their dreams, and how delicious they found the food. They shared a traditional salad made with shredded cabbage, pickled tea leaves, sesame seeds, fried garlic, and roasted peanuts. After that, they shared a dish of spicy shrimp with pickled mango sauce and rice. During the meal, the waiter brought several samples for them to try. Pleasantly satiated, they sipped green tea and munched on guava rice cakes.

At the end of the meal, Charles handed the waiter his Sea Card. They each had a card issued by the cruise line that provided identification, entry to their staterooms, and acted as a credit card everywhere that payment was required on the ship. Their cards came preloaded with $300, which was an incentive for upgrading to the higher-priced balcony rooms.

"You have to let me pay some of the time," Sarah said as they left the restaurant. "I don't want to go home with credit on my card!"

"Might I suggest shopping?" Charles responded playfully.

"You might. But then I might not have room in my suitcase!"

"Then might I suggest buying another suitcase?" he said playfully still, but now also practical.

As they walked down the stairs to the next deck, they saw Matilda coming out of a small sandwich shop carrying a to-go bag that did not appear to be large enough to carry more than one sandwich. "Do you suppose he is eating in their room again?" Sarah asked.

"They sure don't seem to spend much time together," he responded.

"It's a strange marriage." Looking at her watch, she added, "What time does the play start?"

"It doesn't start until 9:00. How about a romantic stroll on the deck?" he asked slyly, reaching for her hand. She giggled, feeling like a youngster in love.

* * * * *

"I just don't know about that Elwood Knowles character," Charles was saying as he and Sarah walked toward the theater later that night. "Something about that man is creepy."

"Creepy?" Sarah teased. "Is that an official law enforcement profile?"

Charles smiled, "Okay, I suppose it's not very specific. I just have a bad feeling about him." When Charles was killing time walking around the ship while Sarah was in class, he had run into Knowles. They spoke briefly, but Knowles seemed to be trying to get away. Charles asked if he would like to sit down in the nearby bar and have a drink. Knowles seemed reluctant but agreed. Charles had hoped to learn more about the man, but even with his highly honed interview skills he wasn't able to learn anything. "What do you think of the wife?"

"She seems tense, but I think that's just because she's learning something new. Tomorrow I'll see if I can get her talking about her husband."

"Maybe we should just stay out of it," Charles suggested.

"You started it, my dear man," Sarah responded. "You're the one that said he's creepy."

As they turned the corner heading toward the theater, they ran into Jeffrey Worme, Sophie's new friend. "Hello," he greeted, a bit reluctantly. "Where are you off to?"

Sarah started talking about the play they were going to see when a very refined woman with a silver-trimmed cane walked toward them. "Jeffrey," she said harshly. "We're going to be late."

"Sorry, dear," Jeffrey apologized. "I would like you to meet two friends of mine. This is Charles Parker and Mrs. Sarah Miller." Turning to the woman with a stiff smile, he continued, "And this is Mrs. Wellington-Hadden. We met in the Hamptons last year."

"Glad to meet you, Mrs. ... Hadden, is it?" Sarah stumbled, not sure what to call her.

"How do you do," was her only response as she looked toward the theater and added, "We are late, Jeffrey." She was dressed in a black crepe evening gown with a diamond necklace that sparkled under the corridor lights. Her hair was meticulously coiffed and a fur stole was casually slung over Jeffrey's arm. "Be careful with that," she demanded, turning toward Jeffrey. "It's about to drag on the floor." She turned and walked away without a word. Jeffrey followed, looking back with an apologetic shrug.

"Well, well," Charles said quietly as the unmatched couple walked away. "What do you suppose that was all about?"

"I have no idea," Sarah responded. "But I sure hope Sophie isn't getting herself into something."

As they entered the theater, Sarah was amazed at the opulence. "I didn't expect this!" She exclaimed, taking in the crystal chandeliers and plush velvet curtains. She was glad she had chosen to wear one of her cocktail dresses. The usher led them to their seats in the orchestra section, and as she sat she was aware of the plush cushioned seats. "This is the ultimate in luxury," she added.

They both enjoyed the play and stood for several curtain calls. As they were leaving their seats, they spotted the Worme / Wellington-Hadden couple heading for the nearby emergency exit. The straight-backed woman was carrying herself as if she owned the theater, and Jeffrey tagged along behind. An usher rushed over to redirect them away from the emergency exit, but the woman totally ignored him and continued through the door with Jeffrey struggling to keep up. Sarah saw him offer his apologetic shrug, this time to the usher.

"Strange," Sarah said contemplatively. "Really strange."

That night, Sarah got into bed around midnight, but she wasn't sleepy. As she laid there thinking about the day, she heard a tap on the door adjoining Sophie's room. She got up and opened it. Sophie stood there in her elephant pajamas.

"Yes, yes, I brought them," she said defensively. "I was afraid I couldn't sleep without them. May I come in?"

"Of course," Sarah said, moving aside.

"I can't sleep. I was wondering if you would like to watch a movie."

"Sounds like fun. Hop in the bed and I'll order popcorn." Sarah responded. The ship's broadcast system was offering several first-run movies, and they chose a comedy.

"I feel like a teenager," Sarah said at one point as they lay in bed giggling and eating popcorn.

"I'm glad you talked me into this trip," Sophie said contritely, thinking about all the fuss she had made about coming. "It's been fun," she added quietly.

"Does that mean you'll come with me to a quilting class?" Sarah asked eagerly.

"Don't push it."

Chapter 17

The next morning there was a tapping at their door early in the morning—at least what felt like early morning. Sarah checked the clock and was surprised to see it was nearly 9:00. "Just a minute," she called out as she fumbled for her robe.

The steward was at the door with a pushcart filled with food. "Breakfast," he announced.

"Did we order breakfast?" she asked, turning to Sophie who had the covers pulled up to her chin.

"Not me, but it sounds good," she responded. "Can we have it even if it isn't ours?" she asked in her serious but joking tone. The steward looked a bit baffled, not knowing what to do. Fortunately, at that moment, Charles stepped out of his room.

"I ordered that," he announced. "Just take it into that room." Turning to Sarah, he asked, "May I join you ladies for breakfast?"

"What can I say, since you provided the food?" she teased. The steward placed the food on their table and Charles returned to his room to get a third chair. While he was gone, Sophie slipped on her robe, and the three had a cozy breakfast of bacon and eggs served with Belgium waffles piled high with fresh strawberries and whipped cream. Twenty minutes later, the steward returned with a second pot of hot coffee.

"Delicious," Sarah swooned, licking her fingers when she finished. Charles smiled at her lovingly and Sophie reached over and snatched Sarah's neglected bacon.

"What's up for today?" Sophie asked as she bit into the bacon.

"I'm free until about 1:30. That's my machine quilting class."

"I thought you were already quilting by machine," Sophie said, looking confused.

"I've been piecing. That's the step where you sew the pieces together to make the quilt top. Quilting is the step where you sew through all the layers to keep them together."

"What layers?" Sophie asked. Sarah was encouraged to see Sophie sounding interested in the process.

"The pieced top, the backing, and the batting in the middle."

"Humph." Sophie said as she reached for Sarah's last piece of bacon, clearly finished with the conversation about quilts.

"So what are we going to do this morning?" Charles asked.

"I want to finish off some hand stitching, but I can carry that with me. What would you like to do, Sophie?"

"I want to go to the casino," she announced with a flair. "I feel lucky today."

"Let's do it!" Sarah responded. "That sounds like fun."

Charles moved the cart into the hall and took his chair back to his room. Sticking his head back in the room he asked, "How much time do you ladies need?"

"We need to take showers and slip into our casino attire. How about we meet you in an hour?" Sarah suggested.

"Perfect. I have some emails to deal with, so tap on my door when you're ready," Charles said as he left the room.

Sarah briefly wondered whom Charles was emailing but didn't ask. In fact, Charles had previously sent a request to his old lieutenant, Matthew Stokely, asking him to run a check on Elwood Knowles. At breakfast, he made a decision to throw Jeffrey Worme into the mix, primarily to make sure Sophie wasn't getting into anything that might backfire on her. He wasn't really worried; he saw Worme as simply a buffoon, but he had a bad feeling about Knowles.

Charles was pleased to see he already had a response from Stokely.

Hey, Charlie!

You are supposed to be vacationing! What's with this Knowles request of yours? I ran it, and this is one boring guy. No record, no warrants, no traffic tickets—nothing of any interest. It seems he worked for an insurance company for a number of years, quit about five years ago, and has been working part-time at Branson's Hardware in Hamilton since then. Boring, as I said. Nothing on his wife at all except they've been married forever. So, what's this all about?

—Matt

Matt,

I have no idea why I'm asking about this guy. Gut feeling. You know how that is. I just don't like the guy and he is hiding something. I guess I should just ignore it. But you know me. Which brings me to my second request. There's this guy who seems to have taken an interest in Sarah's friend, Sophie. I don't have any reason to mistrust the guy but, again, guts. His name is Jeffrey Worme from somewhere back East ... New Hampshire, I think. Would you take a look? Then I'll leave you alone and enjoy my vacation.

—Charles

Later that morning, the three travelers were sitting at adjoining slot machines and lamenting their losses. "Whose silly idea was this anyway?" Sophie complained. But at that moment bells rang and whistles blew—Sophie hit a jackpot! Stewards and fellow gamblers came running. Sophie jumped up and down waving her arms crying, "I did it! I did it!" Charles noticed that Jeffrey was immediately at her side, joining in the celebration.

As it turned out, it was a relatively small jackpot, but Sophie talked like she was "in the money." She strutted around without the use of her cane telling strangers how she did it, taking full credit for what most would say was the luck of the draw. "I knew that machine was a winner! I knew it the minute I laid eyes on it!" she bragged.

Sophie was eager to cash out and have the actual dollars in her hands. She was devastated when they told her it had been credited to her account. "It's on your Sea Card, Sophie," Charles assured her, but she was very disappointed.

"I wanted to hold it," she whined. Jeffrey stayed close by, putting his arm around her and attempting to reassure her. Charles was glad he had sent the request through to Matt.

When Charles returned to his room later that day, Matt had sent a short note.

Charlie,

Are you sure you got the guy's name right? There is no record on him anywhere. Perhaps this is the guy to keep your eye on; forget about the boring Elwood.

—Matt

* * * * *

"Hi, I'm Sandy McFarland." Sarah raised her head, realizing she was bent over the machine with her head practically touching it. She had noticed the young girl sitting at the next machine earlier. She had been machine quilting much faster than Sarah and seemed to already know what she was doing.

"I'm Sarah Miller. You are really good at this! I noticed your machine just flying along and …" Sarah looked over at Sandy's work more closely. "… and you are doing an incredible job! Surely you didn't just learn, did you?"

Sandy laughed. "Actually, I've had three machine quilting classes before this one, but this is the first time I was able to do it. It just all came together for me suddenly."

"I'm having a terrible time," Sarah complained. "I just don't seem to get it. What's your secret?"

"I think it started working for me after I relaxed. My shoulders were up around my ears and my whole body was stiff. When Delores said to shake out all the tension and just relax, it started to work for me. See what I did here? I actually wrote my name!" she said proudly.

Sarah made an attempt to relax her body but noticed that as she approached the project she tensed up again. "Try the quilting gloves," Sandy suggested. Sarah put the rubber-tipped gloves on and started again, but this time trying to stay conscious of her body. Every few minutes she would need to tell herself again to relax as her shoulders crept up and her arms squeezed into her body.

"Relax," Sarah said quietly to herself. "Just *relax*." Suddenly she realized she was actually doing it. Once she found that she could guide the material around under the needle, she started to feel more confident. She stopped to look at her work and realized there were many things to remember. She had relaxed but forgot to control the stitch length. They varied from very tiny to almost an inch long!

Delores stopped at Sarah's machine and asked, "How's it going, Sarah?"

"Well, I managed to get the material to move under the needle just the way I wanted it to, but now I see my stitches are terrible! What am I doing wrong?" she asked.

"You aren't doing a thing wrong, Sarah. You have the idea. From this point on, it's just practice. You will eventually begin to move your fabric at a steady rhythm, and you will find your rhythm, I promise. Sometimes I hum and sway just a little bit looking for that rhythm. Let me see you try it."

Sarah started sewing and humming a slow waltz. "Ah! I see the problem," Delores said softly. "You are going too slowly. You need to speed up the machine and hold it at a steady speed. Try it now but faster."

Sarah pushed harder on the pedal and held it steady while trying to keep the fabric going under the needle in an orderly fashion. Her stitches were now more even, but she had completely lost control of her design. She had been trying to follow the outline of the flowers printed on the fabric. "You aren't going to believe this, Sarah, but you are doing great! It will just take practice."

"That's just what Sandy said. I had hoped to quilt the wallhanging I've been working on with Stephanie, but …"

Delores interrupted, "… let that go. That's just added pressure. Relax and practice. And after you get home, make yourself a pile of sandwiches ready to quilt and pile them by the machine. Whenever you get a chance, practice. Okay?"

"Yes, Delores. Thank you." After Delores walked away, Sarah turned to Sandy and whispered, "*Sandwiches?*"

"She just means two pieces of fabric with batting in the middle. Just do small ones from your scraps and have them ready so you can practice for a few minutes whenever you're on the machine."

Sarah continued working on this new skill, hoping to see some improvement. By the end of the class, she had to admit that her work was already improving.

As she was leaving the work area, Sarah spotted a woman whom she had met in her appliqué class. "Hi," she called. "What's that you're working on?"

The woman held up the block, and Sarah raised both hands to her cheeks. "How charming!" Sarah cried. The block was an adorable little girl wearing a dress, an apron, and a huge bonnet that covered her face, all appliquéd onto a background piece. "Is this a wallhanging?" Sarah asked.

"No, this is little Sunbonnet Sue. I'm going to make twelve of these blocks in different fabrics and use them to make a baby quilt for my new granddaughter," she said proudly. The woman reached for her tote bag and pulled out a picture that had been carefully placed right on the top.

"Oh, she's adorable! And this quilt will be perfect for her. What are these fabrics? They look like fabrics that were in the quilts my mother made when I was a little girl."

"These are 1930s reproduction fabrics. Aren't they sweet?"

"I wonder if I can still get into that class. I would love to make one for my granddaughter."

"Oh!" the woman responded enthusiastically. "You have a granddaughter, too!"

"Well, not yet. My son, Jason, and his new wife are expecting their first baby later this year. This would be such a perfect quilt for her."

"Oh, it's a girl! This would be just right!"

After leaving the workshop, Sarah didn't want to go directly back to the room. She went out on the deck and noticed a deck chair that had been pulled away from the others and offered a bit of privacy. She decided to sit down and relax in the late afternoon sun. Her thoughts went to her son, Jason, and his son, Arthur. Arthur would have been eighteen this year, she realized. The seven years since his death had been hard on the whole family.

At eleven, Arthur had been full of energy and often rode for hours on his bike through the trails in the woodland park behind their house. On that tragic day, he had ridden his bike to his friend Marty's house, and the two boys headed for the park. A white sports car came careening around the corner without stopping at the sign. Two witnesses who were in their front yards saw the car and the boys. One man yelled, "Watch out!" but it was too late. The car struck Arthur head-on and he was killed instantly. It grazed the other boy, causing him to fly off his bike and land near Arthur's body. By the time the neighbors reached them, Marty was laying across Arthur crying and pleading for him to get up. It took two men to pull Marty off of Arthur's body. "Help my friend! Help my friend!" he screamed hysterically. Tears ran down Sarah's cheeks as she recalled the details told to her by the neighbor.

Jason was devastated, of course, but his wife, Joyce, blamed herself and sank into a deep depression. She withdrew from family and friends and spent most of her time in her darkened room. She refused treatment, saying she didn't deserve to live. Jason and Joyce continued to live their silent life, together yet apart. Five years after Arthur's death, Joyce told Jason she was moving to San Antonio to live with her family. He asked if she wanted a divorce, and she said she didn't care. She left the next week without fanfare. She was just gone one day when he came home from work.

Three years later, Jason filed for divorce. He began dating a young woman from his office, but it took another year before he introduced her to the family. He had continued to live in the house he and Joyce had shared. One weekend, he invited Sarah and Martha, his sister, to a cookout to meet Jennifer. Sarah adored Jennifer, but Martha, who was generally negative about any changes, thought she was too young for Jason. Fortunately, Jason put no stock in Martha's opinion and he married Jenny a year later. Martha came to the wedding and even helped Sarah plan the rehearsal dinner, but she never made an effort to get to know Jennifer.

The couple decided to sell the house and start married life in a new home. They bought a new split-level home in a development just a few miles from Sarah. When they told Sarah that Jenny was pregnant, Sarah was overjoyed! She pictured herself pushing the stroller through the park with Barney at her side. As she sat on the deck of the ship, Sarah now pictured the baby wrapped in a beautiful Sunbonnet Sue quilt.

Sarah sighed and got up from the deck chair. *Life goes on.*

"Let's just enjoy our vacation. We have six days left and *so* much more we want to do. Okay?"

"Okay. What's our agenda look like for the next few days?"

"Tomorrow we will be docking in San Juan," she exclaimed looking surprised. "Did you forget that?"

"No, but we never talked about what we would do on the days we are docked. How do you want to play it?"

"I want to watch the cable channel presentation on the land excursion and see what the alternatives are. I never really had a chance to explore that part of the brochures," she responded.

"I know," he chuckled. "All you could talk about was the quilting classes. We never got around to planning our excursions."

"Well, then, let's go do it now!" Charles called for dinner to be delivered to Sarah's room but asked the steward to hold for a moment while he called out to Sarah. "Is Sophie going to be eating with us?"

"No," she hollered from the bathroom where she was styling her windblown hair. "She's out with Jeffrey."

"Um," Charles grunted uncertainly and continued placing the order.

"What was that grunt for?" Sarah asked as she returned to the room.

"Nothing really. Well, maybe I'm just a little concerned for Sophie."

"Don't start, Charles!"

"No, I'm not going to get nuts about it. I just don't know that I trust this Worme guy."

"You don't trust *any* guy, Worme or otherwise."

"That's not true," Charles responded. "It's just that ..."

"It's just what?" she interrupted.

"Well, he latched onto Sophie right away; then we see him with that Wimbledon woman ..."

"Mrs. Wellington-Hadden," Sarah corrected.

"Then yesterday, while you were in class, I saw him at the bar on the Sun deck carrying on with the female wine steward."

"Carrying on? What were they doing?" Sarah asked curiously.

"Just talking, I guess. But they looked pretty friendly ..."

"As I said, Charles, don't start!"

"Okay, okay. I'll stop with Jeffrey Worme. But I'm still keeping my eye on the elusive Elwood."

Their dinner came and was served on the small table in Sarah's room. They adjusted the monitor to the excursions channel and sat down to eat while they watched. Charles totally forgot about Jeffrey and Elwood as he learned about the historical and military sites in San Juan. "We've gotta do this!" he said enthusiastically.

Sarah was particularly interested in the street vendors in Old San Juan and hoped she could find gifts for the girls: her daughter, Martha, and Jason's wife, Jenny.

"When is the baby due?" Charles asked as they were finishing their dessert.

"In about two months, I think. They are hoping she arrives before the holidays. Jason wants to take maternity leave and stay home with Jenny and the baby for a month or so, if possible," Sarah explained.

"How modern of him," Charles responded with the slightest touch of sarcasm in his voice. He was immediately sorry. He saw a disapproving look cross Sarah's face, but it immediately faded. "Sorry," he added. "That was insensitive."

"It's okay." Sarah responded, letting him off the hook. "This whole pregnancy is reminding Jason of his son, Arthur, and the pain of losing him. He just wants to be close by this time."

"I understand," Charles replied, reaching for Sarah's hand. "I know it's hard for you, too." Sarah smiled and threw him an air kiss, letting him know she appreciated his concern. They started the San Juan feature over and made some notes about what they wanted to do on the first day. On the second day, they planned to take a bus tour outside of town to see Puerto Rico beyond the city.

Charles was particularly interested in the Río Camuy Cave Park, but Sarah was reluctant. Being willing to try most anything, she knew she would agree to the caves if Charles seemed really interested, but she wasn't eager to descend deep into the earth in a foreign land. She was just a little claustrophobic but didn't want to let that keep her from doing what she wanted to do.

Sarah also suggested the El Yunque rain forest, and he liked that idea, too. They enjoyed walking together and the trails and waterfalls looked intriguing in the film. "We don't have to sign up until that morning. Let's just wait and see how we feel about it then," Charles suggested.

"Good plan," Sarah agreed. As they were standing, Sophie burst into the room in a flurry.

"That man! He must know every woman on this ship!" she complained.

"Are we talking about Jeffrey?" Charles asked with mock innocence, tossing Sarah just the suggestion of an "I told you so" look.

"We are talking about *The Worm*," Sophie snapped. "That's spelled *w-o-r-m*!"

"What happened?" Sarah asked, frowning at Charles. She didn't have Charles' tendency to see crime at every turn, but on the other hand she was very protective of her special friend and didn't want her getting hurt.

"Well, it's not that anything happened, exactly. It's just that one woman after another came up to the table all night and most of them were flirting shamelessly." Sophie frowned and added, "In fact, *all* of them were flirting, except maybe this one ritzy dame with a whole line of names."

"Did Jeffrey flirt back?" Sarah asked.

"Well, no. Not exactly. But my question is this: How does he know so many women already? We've only been at sea three days!" Immediately changing the subject, she looked at all the notes on the table and asked, "What's going on here?"

"We were planning our days in San Juan. Let's go over the plan and see what you think of it," Sarah responded. They turned the excursion channel back on and fast-forwarded to the side trips.

"I'm not interested in either one of those. Too much walking for me! Jeffrey is talking about wanting to see the Bacardí rum distillery. They have a tour that I think I could manage. Then he thinks we can find a tour of the city by bus or cab, or even by horse and buggy," she added with a mischievous grin. Charles and Sarah exchanged a private look, both hoping Sophie wasn't going to get hurt.

"Jeffrey has some sort of business in San Juan in the morning, and he said he will meet up with us around noon, so I'll go with you guys in the morning, okay?"

"Of course! We hoped you would be with us all day," Sarah said.

"*Pa-leeez!*" Sophie responded, tossing her head back arrogantly. "I *do* have a life, you know."

Chapter 19

ater that night, Sarah heard thunder in the distance and the room was momentarily aglow from lightening. There was a tapping on the door adjoining Sophie's room. "Should I be worried?" Sophie asked as Sarah opened the door.

"No. This is perfectly normal. Come on in and stay with me if you want. It will be over soon. They're predicting a warm sunny day in San Juan tomorrow."

But the thunder sounded closer and more frequent, and the lightening became almost continuous. Sarah pulled the drapes back and was mesmerized by the streaks of light flashing across the sky. Looking down at the water, she could see white caps surrounding the ship. The ship began rolling so violently that Sarah stumbled attempting to return to her bed.

"You told me this was a floating hotel! I don't feel like we're floating ..."

"Sophie, relax. It's just a little storm," Sarah said, reassuring her roommate that they were safe. "Just lie down and relax."

Sarah wasn't as confident as she sounded, and she wished Charles would come to the door. She hesitated to call him this late. Still, she needed some reassurance herself. The ship was rocking back and forth violently, and several times the lights had flickered as if they were losing power. She wondered what would happen if the ship lost power but then decided there was probably a backup generator, like she and Jonathan had when the kids were young.

She thought about the storm that struck Middletown in 1973. She was pregnant with Jason, and Martha was only two. It had started with a routine thunderstorm, but suddenly it sounded as if a freight train were heading right for their house. Not knowing what to do, they all laid flat on the floor, Sarah covering Martha protectively and Jonathan enveloping them both in his arms. Since then, she learned that they should have moved to the basement where there were no windows.

The tornado hit their neighborhood, barely skimming past their house. When they dared to go outside, they found their neighbor's house essentially gone and the houses across the street severely damaged. Neighbors stood around speechless, probably in shock. Sarah's beloved garden remained intact, as did the picket fence Jonathan had built to enclose her precious flowers. She would have given them all up to the storm if it would have saved the lives of the elderly couple next door. It had been a bad year for storms, and Jonathan bought the generator to make sure they had electricity when the baby arrived.

There was a light tapping on the other door. Sarah slipped her robe on and made her way across the room, holding onto furniture. "Are you okay?" Charles asked when she opened it.

"We're fine," she responded. He looked over and saw Sophie's eyes peeking over the covers that she had pulled up to her nose.

"I'm not sure we needed three rooms," he said laughing. "I see you have a roommate again tonight."

"We were both scared." Sophie's voice was muffled by the covers.

Sarah turned the bedside lamp on and sat down on the love seat. "I'm glad you two are together," Charles said as he sat next to her.

"If this is truly a floating hotel, ask the doorman to hail me a cab." Sophie tried to sound at ease, but Charles and Sarah could both hear the tension in her voice.

"Do you want to get up and have a drink?" Charles asked, looking toward Sophie. He had a bottle in his hand. Without waiting for an answer, he headed for the bathroom, where he collected three wrapped water glasses. Sophie slipped cautiously out of the bed and Sarah saw that she was still wearing her robe. The two women moved to the chairs and wrapped the extra blankets around themselves. It wasn't cold, but they both felt more secure that way. Charles sat down near them on the love seat after pouring them each a shot of bourbon.

Sophie took a gulp and spewed it across the room. "What's that vile stuff?" she demanded.

"Here, let me add some coke to what you have left," Charles offered, opening the mini refrigerator and removing two of the cokes they had placed there earlier.

"Well, that's somewhat better," Sophie admitted after taking a cautious sip.

"Surely that wasn't your first taste of bourbon," Sarah teased.

"You're right," she admitted, "but it's the first in many years. I guess I had younger taste buds in those days. Anyway, it's not bad with coke. Can I have a little more?" Sophie asked timidly. "It's really warm going down."

The three sat talking and enjoying their drinks, momentarily forgetting about the storm—that is, until an enormous wave lifted the ship high in the air and dropped it abruptly with a crash that caused both women to scream and sent Sophie onto the floor. Charles scrambled to help Sophie up. Together, Sarah and Charles guided her to the bed. While Sarah checked her over, making sure nothing was broken, Charles retrieved the bottle and glasses that had scattered across the floor. "I'll call for the steward," he said.

"Why don't we wait until after the storm?" Sarah suggested. "I'm sure they have lots on their mind right now."

Five decks up on the Mercury deck, where the exclusive balcony suites were located, one suite sat empty. The French doors to the balcony stood open, and the curtains blew back into the room violently. The balcony chairs were overturned. The radio was softly playing big band music from the 40s. "The sweetest music this side of heaven," Matilda had often said.

Charles stayed until after 3:00 a.m., when the sea settled down. Sophie fell asleep around 2:00, and Charles and Sarah talked softly until Sarah, too, finally began to nod. He led her to the bed, covered them both, and tiptoed quietly out of the room.

About the same time up on the Mercury deck, Matilda was calling for the steward. "I'm sorry to bother you so late, but I need help with something."

"No problem," the steward responded. "I'm on night duty. I'll be right up."

When he arrived at the Knowles suite, Matilda pointed to the open French doors. "I can't get these to close tight. Can you help me?"

"Were they open through that terrible storm?" he asked incredulously.

"I don't know. I stayed down in the Jupiter lounge through most of it. It was like this when I came up." Before closing the doors, he turned the balcony deck chairs upright and then secured the French doors.

"They seem fine," he said, examining the locking mechanism. "Just keep them locked if we have another storm."

Matilda smiled proudly as she prepared for bed. *Calling for that guy was a stroke of genius!*

Chapter 20

Early the next morning, Charles and Sarah made their way to one of their favorite breakfast restaurants, feeling the need for a hearty breakfast before they started out on their day's excursion. They chose a table by the window where they could watch for dolphins. They were approaching the islands and had been told the sea life was very active in these waters.

"Isn't that your friend Matilda sitting in the corner alone?" Charles asked. Sarah turned to look and the woman immediately dropped her eyes to avoid Sarah's.

"Yes, that's Matilda. She doesn't seem to want me to notice her, though." Sarah turned back toward Charles and continued eating. She was becoming addicted to the Belgium waffles stacked high with fresh berries and globs of whipped cream. Today she had them with blueberries and closed her eyes with each bite, wallowing in the decadent pleasure.

"We rarely see them together. Do you suppose there is trouble in that marriage?"

"Who?" Sarah asked, having been completely distracted from their conversation by the food.

"Matilda and Elwood."

"Charles! That's none of our business," Sarah responded, shaking her head as if she couldn't believe he was at it again. "You are such a busybody!"

"It's just strange …" he started to say.

"We don't know what's strange for them. Maybe they never eat together!" Sarah interjected. "As a matter of fact, I'm not sure I've ever seen them having a meal together. But who knows about other people's habits. Eat your breakfast and get your nose out of their affairs." She then added with a coy smile, "Concentrate on your own *affairs*." He winked, not knowing how else to respond.

They had been dancing around the subject of intimacy for the past year. Sarah had clearly only wanted a friendship in the beginning, despite the fact that he was head over heels in love with her. But lately he noticed a flirtatious tone in her voice, as if she were sending him a message. He was no good at interpreting subtle messages when they were coming from Sarah. She reached over and touched his hand. He noticed she held his eyes a little longer than usual before she shyly dropped them. *The secret language of women*, he thought. *I'll never understand.*

Charles had been married to one woman since high school. She died following a long, drawn-out illness that drained them both of all energy. After her death, he concentrated on his job and never thought about dating. At least, not until he met the lovely Sarah Miller. The day she walked into that coffee shop three years earlier, his heart took a tumble and had been tumbling ever since. He winked at her again.

What was that look? she wondered.

Before they had finished their meal, Sophie came hobbling into the restaurant. She was using her cane and appeared to be in pain. "Sophie, over here," Sarah called. Sophie continued to their table and let out a deep sigh as she plopped into the chair.

"Phew. That was no easy trip!"

"What's the matter? Did you fall again?" Sarah asked, seeing that Sophie was limping more than usual.

"No, it's just my arthritis acting up. Just part of getting old," she added, looking pitiful as she scanned their faces for signs of sympathy.

"It was probably that fall you took last night. Is your ankle really okay?"

"Fiddlesticks!"

"I'll assume that means you didn't injure your ankle. So are you going to feel like going into San Juan today?"

"I wouldn't miss it!" she responded enthusiastically, forgetting about her quest for sympathy. "But I'm not going with you two. I'm going to wait here for Jeffrey. He's arranging for a cab to pick us up at noon."

About that time, Jeffrey walked into the restaurant. Sophie waved her hand, but he didn't see her. He was hesitantly looking in the direction of Matilda. He started toward her table, but she waved him away with an almost imperceptible movement of her hand. Sarah and Charles both noticed it, however, and looked at each other.

"He knows Matilda, too?" Charles whispered, giving Sarah a look that said he might be right to mistrust the guy.

"Don't start," Sarah said quietly, hoping Sophie hadn't noticed any of it.

"Don't start what?" Sophie asked.

"He's just being a cop, Sophie. Ignore him."

Sophie placed her breakfast order and was talking about their plans for the day as Jeffrey approached the table. "Join us?" Charles offered.

"Don't mind if I do," Jeffrey responded, glancing over his shoulder at Matilda.

"I understand you have business in San Juan today," Charles said casually.

"Yes, but only a couple of hours."

Charles wanted to pursue the topic; in fact, he wanted to ask the nature of the business, but he knew Sarah would be upset with him for prying. He just looked at Jeffrey, waiting for details that never came. As Jeffrey placed his order, Charles noticed his hair sparkled a little blacker than the day before. *A fresh application of shoe polish*, Charles thought with a smile.

* * * * *

As the ship approached Puerto Rico, the three friends stood on the deck astounded by the beauty. White sands extended from the land out into the bluest of waters. "Maybe we made a mistake signing up for those tours. The beaches are breathtaking!" Sarah said.

"Do you want to cancel our land excursions?" Charles asked obligingly. "We can spend the day on the beach if you would like."

"No. Let's save the beach for when we get to St. Thomas," Sarah responded.

As the ship approached the harbor, the landscape changed from palm trees on white beaches to a modern city with high-rises. "I didn't expect this," Sophie said. "This looks like Chicago!" As they were watching the slow approach to the island, the loud speaker sputtered and the captain's voice blasted across the deck.

"Attention all passengers. There has been a change in our itinerary. We will not be discharging passengers at San Juan port at this time. I repeat: We will *not* be discharging passengers at San Juan port. Local officials will be boarding the ship for the purpose of conducting an investigation. Please extend your complete cooperation with these officials. Please return to your cabins and turn on your monitors. Additional information will be provided as it becomes available. We apologize for the inconvenience."

As the passengers roamed around the deck, watching for the officials and speculating as to what was happening, Sarah looked toward the railing about twenty feet away, where Matilda stood staring out across the water. Two ship employees appeared at her side and led her toward the staff elevator that went directly to the bridge. Matilda appeared to be unsteady as she leaned against one of the men for support. Sarah, looking astounded, turned to Charles and said, "What do you suppose that is all about?" Looking up just as Matilda was getting off the elevator on the top deck, she added, "Is that the captain up there?"

"Yes," he responded, turning in time to see the captain greet Matilda and lead her into his office.

The ship had docked and the gangplank had been dropped. Dozens of armed police officers from San Juan began boarding the ship. "We should head for our cabins," Charles said. "Where's Sophie?"

At that moment, Sophie approached looking upset. "Jeffrey said it was essential that he get off the ship. He wouldn't tell me why. I think he's going to try to slip past the guards."

"Guards?" Sarah asked looking confused. "What guards?"

"Look down there by the gangplank," Sophie said, pointing toward the dock. Half a dozen San Juan police officers were blocking the gangplank, breaking rank only to let additional officials board the ship.

About that time, three black SUVs pulled up and men in black suits quickly headed toward the gangplank. The guards parted, letting them through. "FBI," Charles said with astonishment. "What are they doing here?" he muttered to himself. Looking toward the bow, Charles caught sight of Jeffrey disappearing down a stairwell marked "Authorized Personnel Only."

"Please return to your staterooms immediately." The voice on the loudspeaker blasted once and then repeated the message at one-minute intervals until the deck was cleared. Charles and Sarah headed for the elevator, but she tugged at his shirt indicating she wanted to take the steps. "It's a long way up, sweetie," he said.

"I know, but look," she responded pointing toward the dock. He realized what she was doing. From the vantage point of the metal stairway, they were able to see the activity on the dock and around the gangplank.

As they reached the next deck, they turned to see three military vans pulling up to the dock. Hordes of men and women in uniform climbed out and rushed toward the gangplank. The guards stepped aside, allowing them to board the ship. Within seconds, military personnel were swarming throughout the ship. Charles and Sarah moved back against the wall as a dozen or so hurried up the metal stairs and immediately fanned out. At a distance, they could see others ascending stairs to the upper decks. "We should be in our room," Charles said. "They're searching the ship."

Suddenly small aircraft flew over their heads and out to sea, following the path taken by the ship as it approached land the night before. "Search planes," Charles said with a frown. Coast guard boats were making ready and leaving their slips, headed in the same direction as the planes. "They're looking for something! That's for sure," Charles added thoughtfully.

"Do you suppose someone fell overboard?" Sarah asked.

Hurrying on up the stairs to the Saturn deck, they headed for Sarah's room. Once inside, Charles immediately turned the monitor on and opened the connecting door to his room so he could hear if anyone knocked.

"What happened to Sophie?" Sarah asked, surprised that she wasn't already in her room.

"I don't know. She was behind us, and then she veered off, probably toward the elevator," he responded. "Let's leave her door open as well so we'll know when she comes in." They pulled their chairs up so they could easily view the monitor. There was a scrolling message instructing everyone to stay in their stateroom until further notice and stating that additional information would be posted when it was available.

"What do you suppose this is all about?" Sarah asked Charles. She looked worried, and he reached over and touched her cheek.

"Don't worry, sweetie. We'll find out soon enough." He didn't want to say anything that would upset or frighten her, but in watching the action, he had originally suspected there might be a fugitive aboard. He thought the men had boarded the ship in a manner resembling the way SWAT teams might have boarded, but he didn't see any firearms. But now, seeing the planes and coast guard search and rescue boats, he didn't know what to think. *Maybe they're looking for a fugitive who they think might have jumped off the ship*, he speculated, but decided that was a bit far-fetched.

It was a half hour later when Sophie came in. She tapped at Sarah's door, but before they could open it, she came in through her own room. "I have some information," she said, looking excited and eager to share her news. "I ran into our steward down the hall. He wasn't supposed to tell me anything, but I finally got it out of him." She smiled proudly and started to walk back into her own room.

"Stop right there," Sarah demanded! "You can't say that and walk away! What's going on?"

"Well, first I need to use the *girls' room*." She continued into her own room and left them waiting for the information she was tantalizing them with. Before she returned, however, the face of the captain appeared on the monitor. As he began talking, Sophie came back into the room looking disappointed. She clearly was looking forward to getting the most out of the information she was holding.

"Did he already tell you?" she asked.

"Tell us what?" Sarah demanded, becoming impatient.

Charles shushed them both as the captain began to speak. He first apologized for the inconvenience. Then he said there was an investigation going on and that an officer would be coming to each room asking for any information the passengers might have. "I request that you be entirely open and honest with the investigators and that you share any and all information you might have regarding the matter."

"What matter?" Sarah said, annoyed that the captain wasn't being more forthcoming.

Stepping to the right, another man took the captain's place in front of the camera. "I am Agent Barlow of the FBI. Your captain has requested your full cooperation. I regret that I must *demand* your full cooperation. Anyone withholding information will be considered impeding an FBI investigation and will be subject to prosecution." The man stepped abruptly to the side, and both faces were replaced by the previous scrolling message that instructed passengers to remain in their staterooms until further notice.

"What investigation?" Sarah demanded of the monitor. "Why are they being so cryptic?"

Sophie had returned to the room and was seated on the love seat, smiling her Cheshire cat smile. "Sophie?" Sarah said, eager for whatever information she had. "What's going on?"

"Elwood Knowles is missing."

Chapter 21

By midafternoon, all staterooms had been searched and everyone had been questioned. Anyone knowing Elwood or Matilda Knowles had been sent to the auditorium to be interviewed by an FBI agent. Everyone else was told they could go ashore, but they would need their Sea Card and a photo ID in order to leave the ship. Two FBI agents were posted at the gangplank, and passenger's identifications were checked as they exited the ship.

As Sarah and Charles sat in the back of the auditorium waiting for their interviewer, Sarah shook her head and said, "I don't know how they managed to process all these people in such a short time. They don't have that many investigators onboard."

Charles mused on this and finally said, "Well, we were outside when the vans from the military base arrived. We saw the local police and the FBI arrive, but once we went inside, we really don't know how many others might have come onboard."

"True," Sarah acknowledged.

"And they were using cruise ship employees for some of the searching," Charles added.

"True." Sarah sat quietly wondering where Sophie was. She had been interviewed briefly and released. She told Sarah she was going to go look for Jeffrey to see if he still wanted to go ashore.

Charles was still wondering what had become of Jeffrey. He was escaping down the back exit when Charles last saw him. He hadn't mentioned this to Sophie or Sarah.

He also hadn't mentioned the argument he had stumbled into the previous day. Charles had just turned a corner when he happened upon Elwood and Jeffrey arguing in hushed tones. Elwood had been reprimanding Jeffrey for his *dalliances*. Charles had thought that was a strange thing for one man to say to another, and for a moment he had wondered about the relationship between these two men. But he had immediately dismissed the thought. They had stopped arguing as Charles approached and had greeted him. Despite his attempts to hide his emotions, Elwood had looked extremely angry. His face had been flushed and his eyes dark. Jeffrey, on the other hand, had seemed relieved by the interruption and had casually invited Charles to a nearby bar for a drink. Charles had declined and continued on his way. As he walked away, he had wondered if perhaps Elwood had caught Jeffrey flirting with Matilda.

Still waiting for the FBI agent, Charles pondered over all the inconsistencies he had observed around Elwood and his sudden disappearance. Jeffrey obviously had some sort of relationship with the man. His devoted wife, Matilda, didn't seem so devoted considering the offhand insults she regularly tossed his way. Professionally, Elwood had said he did "not much of anything," while his wife said he worked all the time. He spoke rarely, avoided people, and reminded Charles of someone, but he wasn't sure of whom.

Charles wondered how much of this he should report to the FBI investigator. They were all just suppositions on his part. He had no proof of anything and no idea what might have become of Elwood. And if the elusive Jeffrey had anything to do with Elwood's disappearance, that was another whole ball of wax. Jeffrey seemed to be in some sort of relationship with the haughty Mrs. Wellington-Hadden of the Hamptons, the wine steward, perhaps Matilda, their own Sophie, and Elwood himself! Beyond that, he had mysterious business in San Juan and had fled when the ship was being boarded by law enforcement. *Again, suppositions.* He decided not to make any decisions about what to report and just let the conversation with the FBI flow naturally. He would know what to say when the time came, he was sure.

He looked at Sarah sitting beside him. She didn't seem to be worried about what to say or what not say to the investigators. She was, however, very upset that they wouldn't let her speak to Matilda. "She has no one!" Sarah had said. "I'm the only person she knows on the ship. I need to be with her."

Always concerned, Charles thought, looking at the worry lines that had appeared on her face. *Always there to help others.* He would attempt to intervene with the investigators and request that she be allowed to see Matilda. He decided to wait until he was being questioned and bring up the issue then.

A local police officer from San Juan approached them and asked, "Are you Sarah Miller?"

"Yes," she replied, looking apprehensive.

"Mrs. Knowles would like to see you. Have you met with the FBI yet?"

"No. I'm waiting now."

"Okay," the officer replied. "I'm going to take you to see Agent Barlow and you will then be taken to Mrs. Knowles' stateroom. Is that okay with you?"

"Absolutely! I'm very worried about her. She's all alone …" she started to say, but the officer was clearly not listening. He led her to the small office area where interviews were taking place.

"What was that all about?" the man sitting across from Charles asked. Charles had not noticed the man until then. He had an olive complexion, dark brown eyes, and appeared to be in his late twenties. He spoke with an accent that Charles didn't recognize. He thought the question was intrusive.

"They just want to talk with her," he responded dismissively.

"Didn't he say something about taking her to Mrs. Knowles?"

"Perhaps." Charles wondered why he was being interrogated by this stranger.

The man continued talking, asking Charles about his profession and where he was from. When the man came to questions about Sarah and her connection to Matilda, Charles cut him short. "Look. I don't know what this is all about, but I'm not interested in talking." The man didn't respond; Charles stood and walked away.

* * * * *

Charles and Sarah presented their Sea Cards and their driver's licenses to the agent clearing passengers to go ashore. They waited while the agent checked the list of passengers who had been authorized to leave the ship. "You have people who *aren't* allowed to leave the ship?" Charles asked.

"You bet, detective."

"Detective? How did you know I'm a detective?" Charles asked, surprised. "Actually a retired detective," he added.

"It's here on my roster. Also, I have a message for you from Agent Barlow. He and the captain would like to meet with you early tomorrow morning. Is 0700 okay with you?"

"It's perfect," he responded. Turning to Sarah, he said, "That way we can get an early start in the morning. Does that work for you?" She was hesitant and frowning. "What is it?" he asked, forgetting the agent was there.

"It's Matilda. I want to see her in the morning."

"Do you want to stay on the ship now and go see her?" he asked.

"No, the ship's doctor gave her something to help her sleep. She'll be okay until morning. Maybe I'll go see her while you're with the captain in the morning, and then we can decide what to do with our day."

"Good idea." Charles added, "For now, let's just take a cab into San Juan and walk around until dinner time. Maybe get dinner on the island. Okay?" he asked, pulling her close and wrapping his arms around her.

She loved his protective hugs, especially when she was upset or worried. *How did I get along without his hugs all those many years?*

Charles decided not to discuss their interviews with the FBI until later. They had been under a great deal of stress all day, and it was time for some fun. They took a cab the short distance to Old San Juan and spent the late afternoon walking up and down the streets, marveling at the architecture, and visiting the small shops and street vendors. Sarah was thankful for her comfortable shoes but sorry she hadn't worn a sundress. She had checked the temperature before leaving the ship but, aside from an occasional breeze from the water, they were hot.

With all the hills, narrow sidewalks, and uneven walking surfaces, Sarah was glad that Sophie had decided not to come into San Juan with them. Her ankle had gotten worse after walking to and from the auditorium that morning.

As if he had read her thoughts, Charles said, "I'm glad Sophie isn't trying to navigate these walkways."

"I agree. She and Jeffrey are going to take a bus tour of the city tomorrow after he finishes with his business in San Juan," Sarah responded. "That will be easier on her."

"What business could he possibly have in San Juan?" Charles finally asked. He had been holding back on this subject for two days and couldn't wait any longer. "Who has business on an island far from home?"

"I don't know, Charles." Trying not to sound as exasperated as she felt, Sarah added, "People have many different lifestyles and not many people live the sedate lives we have in the Midwest and especially in our community. We're accustomed to being around retired people with what some might consider *small lives*. I don't think we should judge him. We really don't know anything about him."

"That's what I'm afraid of," Charles responded. Sarah sighed and Charles dropped the subject.

"Oh, look!" Sarah said excitedly, pointing toward a street vendor's table covered with jewelry that sparkled in the sunshine. They walked over to the vendor and found a spot among the people crowding around the table. "That piece would be perfect for Jenny. The blue matches her eyes." Sarah reached across the table and picked up a delicate necklace with a round lapis stone in a shade of blue as deep as the water surrounding the island. "It's just perfect!"

Charles reached for his wallet, but Sarah laid her hand on his arm. "No, Charles. I want to pay for this." He looked disappointed until she added, "But you can get me something if you would like." She batted her eyelashes in an exaggerated way and gave him a coy look that made him laugh. He began looking through the items on the table and picked up a bracelet, gold with small gemstones in assorted colors.

"This would go with everything, right?" he said to her, showing her the bracelet.

"Yes, it would," she responded. "But so would that," she added, pointing to a very simple bracelet made of thin woven strands of silver. She had spotted the price tag on both items and didn't want him to spend so much on her.

Charles picked up the silver bracelet when he spotted a very ornate necklace. He put the bracelet in his left hand and reached for the necklace. "Oh, Charles, that's so heavy I wouldn't be able to stand up straight!" she laughed. As she moved closer to him, she noticed the man next to Charles slip an item surreptitiously into his pocket. The vendor saw it at the same time as Sarah.

The vendor began yelling for the police. "*Policía! Policía! Ayúdenme!*" The man turned to get away, but a police officer standing nearby was able to grab his arm. The officer asked the vendor what was going on. "*Qué es lo que está pasando?*"

The vendor responded, telling the police officer that the man was stealing from him. "*Este hombre me está robando*," he said over and over.

Laying the jewelry he was holding back on the table, Charles slowly backed away from the vendor, asking Sarah to do the same. "This is not very civic-minded of me, especially since I spent years enforcing the law, but I just don't want to be stuck here as a witness. What do you think of the idea that you and I get out of here?"

"I've had my fill of witnessing for the day. Let's skedaddle," she said with a giggle.

"*Skedaddle?*" Charles repeated, looking surprised. "*Skedaddle?* I haven't heard that word since I visited my grandma's farm some sixty years ago! How did you come up with that?"

"It's a word from my childhood. It just came to me," she said with a melancholy smile. Meanwhile, they were in fact skedaddling, and Charles raised his arm to signal for a cab. A passing taxi screeched to a halt and the two enjoyed a harrowing ride, this time across the bridge and into the modern city of San Juan.

Chapter 22

"This day turned out to be better than I expected," Sarah said as they walked up the gangplank arm in arm. It was nearly midnight, and there was a full moon glistening on the water. A soft breeze tussled Charles' hair, and she pushed it back off his forehead. "It certainly didn't start out very well, but it was fun being on the island with you." They had enjoyed a leisurely dinner in the heart of San Juan and had strolled through the main streets, looking in the shop windows. "I wish we were going to be here longer."

Once on the ship, Charles led her to a deck chair on the ocean side, and they sat down to look out over the glittering water. "I want to talk to you about earlier before we go up," he said gently, reaching for her hand.

"I know."

"I want to tell you about my interview today. I said things you won't be happy about."

"I know. You had to."

Confused by her reaction, he continued. "I told them about my misgivings."

"I probably will, too," she said simply.

"You will?" he was surprised. "You're going to talk to them about Worme?"

She looked surprised. "No. I think I should talk with them about Matilda."

"Matilda? What about her?" Charles was confused. "Tell me."

"When I went to her room this morning after my interview, she was extremely upset. She was pacing around between the room and the balcony and she seemed very nervous."

"That seems normal under the circumstances," Charles said. "Her husband is missing."

"It wasn't that," Sarah responded, looking concerned. "It was her words. First of all, she talked about him as if he were dead."

"You don't think he is?"

"Maybe. Maybe not. That certainly wasn't my first thought. With his blood sugar problems and his obvious frailty, I figured he had passed out somewhere and they would find him. She seemed to *know* he was dead. There was apparently no doubt in her mind. She told me he *obviously* fell off the balcony into the ocean." Sarah looked out across the ocean thoughtfully. "Also, I was surprised that she seemed to have already moved on."

"What do you mean?" Charles asked frowning.

"She was talking about whether she should sell the house and where she might go. She talked about Wisconsin and that perhaps she would move back there. It just didn't fit, Charles. It just didn't feel right."

"Do you think she did something to him?"

"I don't know what I think, Charles."

They were both quiet for a few minutes when she abruptly turned to him, saying, "You wanted to tell me something. What was it?"

"I wanted to tell you that I talked to Agent Barlow about my misgivings regarding Jeffrey Worme. And I told him something I haven't told you yet."

"What's that?" she asked, turning on the deck chair so she was facing him.

He told her about the altercation between Elwood Knowles and Jeffrey in the corridor. "At first I didn't understand it, but now I'm thinking Knowles must have thought there was something going on between Jeffrey and Matilda."

"Why would he think that?" Sarah asked.

"*We* thought it, didn't we? So why wouldn't Knowles?" Charles pointed out. "Besides, Jeffrey probably gave it away. He isn't inclined toward subtlety."

"But you do think he *is* inclined toward murder?" she responded skeptically.

"Yes. No. I don't know, but I talked to Barlow about my concerns. I thought he should know."

"… And I guess I should talk to him about my concerns," Sarah said hesitantly.

"I guess so. But go see Matilda in the morning. She might have just been in shock. I find it hard to believe she is involved in his disappearance."

"… And you don't find it hard to believe that Jeffrey was?" she asked, not willing to let it go. She was primarily thinking about Sophie and what it would mean for the first man she had shown any interest in to be placed under suspicion.

Not wanting to end the day with bad feelings, he put his arm around her and they silently walked up the two flights of stairs to the Neptune deck. The moonlight threw shadows across the deck and through the open metal stairs, occasionally fluttering across Sarah's face. Charles, filled with love, pulled her close and kissed her forehead. She turned her face up to him, and with only a moment's hesitation, they melted into a tender kiss. "Until tomorrow," he said as he opened the door to her stateroom and stepped aside so she could enter. They both hesitated. The moment was electrified until she broke the spell, whispering, "Good night," and gently closing the door.

"Well, that was touching!" Sarah jumped, shocked to find Sophie in her bed.

"What are you doing in here?" she asked, trying to sound annoyed. She was actually glad she wouldn't be alone.

"Never mind that. You two are getting pretty touchy-feely, aren't you? I was about to dive under the bed!"

"Let it go, Sophie. I don't want to talk about it now."

"You never want to talk about it. Are you in love with the guy or not?"

"He's very special," Sarah responded as she hung her dress on a hanger and pulled her robe off the hook.

"That's not an answer."

"I know."

They remained quiet for a few moments until Sophie said, "If you want my advice …"

"Not now, Sophie. Please, not now."

Sophie heard the catch in Sarah's voice and realized she was upset. She wished Sarah could just relax and enjoy her relationship with this very special man, but she knew it would have to come in its own time. "May I stay?" she asked meekly.

"Of course you may stay, Sophie. I don't want to be alone tonight, either."

* * * * *

They were in a deep sleep when Charles tapped on the door early the next morning. Sarah slipped on her robe and opened the door, shushing Charles so he wouldn't wake Sophie. "I'm off to meet with Barlow," he said. "I'm sorry I woke you. Do you want me to stop by when I'm finished?"

"Yes. Wait! I'm going to dress and go check on Matilda. How about we meet at the breakfast buffet when we're both finished?"

"Good plan. I'll see you there." He leaned in and kissed her cheek and started to leave but stuck his head back in. "Did Sophie see Jeffrey yesterday?"

"Oh. I forgot to ask."

He sighed and left for the bridge.

"I'm glad you're here, detective," the captain said as Charles entered the room. Agent Barlow was there with two other FBI agents Charles had met the previous day. They greeted one another and offered Charles coffee, which he eagerly accepted.

"Just call me Charles. I'm retired and not actively a detective anymore," Charles explained.

"Retired or not, your lieutenant told me you're good at what you do."

"You talked to Matthew?"

"You bet I did. Barlow here told me about the conversation you stumbled into between Knowles and Worme. Would you repeat it for us?" Charles told the story a third time while the men listened attentively.

"You think this Worme guy might have reason to kill Knowles?"

"I'm not saying that at all," Charles responded. "I'm simply telling you what I heard. I never saw Worme with Knowles' wife exactly, but we did observe him the morning after Knowles disappeared. She was in the restaurant and he started to walk toward her. She discreetly waved him off. Wait a minute!" he said suddenly, interrupting himself. "What was she doing in the restaurant having breakfast the morning after her husband went missing?"

"We asked her about that. It seems she didn't realize he was gone right away. She went to bed and assumed he was out. It wasn't until after she had breakfast that she began to suspect he was gone," Barlow explained.

"Hmm." Charles appeared to be thinking about this. "Where did she think he spent the night?"

"She just dismissed the question, didn't offer an opinion."

Charles then asked, "What does she think happened to him?"

"She thinks he fell overboard during the storm."

"Is that possible? Where was she during the storm?" Charles asked.

"She was in the lounge part of the time. That's confirmed," one of the other agents answered.

"I would like for you to hear what the passenger in the next stateroom has to say." The captain walked to a side door and opened it. "Please come in, Mr. Hawkins." A short chubby man in a flowered shirt and Bermuda shorts walked in wearing flip-flops. "Tell us what you heard, Mr. Hawkins."

"Arguing," Hawkins began. "Loud arguing. I was closing my balcony door when I heard them yelling."

"Who?" Charles asked.

"I don't know. A man and a woman. They were very angry. I think she was accusing him of something. 'Womanizing,' it sounded like she said."

"Was this before the storm?"

"No. More like during it, but once my balcony door was closed I couldn't hear anymore with the storm and all," he said apologetically. He then added, "Oh, I heard the steward knock on the door much later. It was the middle of the night. I don't know why he was there, but he didn't come to my door. Did you talk to him?"

"Thank you, Mr. Hawkins." The captain led the man back out and talked to him briefly in the corridor. "I told him he could leave the ship. I hope you were finished with him," he said returning to the room and looking at Barlow.

"For now. Sure."

"Did you talk to the steward?" Charles asked, getting really interested.

"Yes. He said Mrs. Knowles called him around 3:00 in the morning to help her close the balcony doors. He found the deck chairs askew but nothing else. That wouldn't be unexpected considering the winds. He said Mr. Knowles wasn't there."

"Was there a problem with the doors? Why couldn't she close them?"

"The steward didn't find a problem. Maybe the wind made it difficult for her," the captain offered.

"Or maybe she needed a witness," Charles said thoughtfully.

"A witness to what?" Sarah asked him later when they met for breakfast. He was telling her what had transpired during his meeting with the captain and the agents.

"A witness to see that she found the doors wide open when she returned from the lounge," he responded, rubbing his forehead. "A witness who might confirm the possibility that Elwood Knowles fell overboard during the storm."

"Hmm," she responded in a noncommittal tone.

"I need to get off this ship and clear my head. But first tell me what you found when you went to see Matilda."

"Nothing. She wasn't in her room." They finished their breakfast in silence.

After eating, they headed back to their rooms to get ready to go ashore. "Is there any word on Jeffrey?" she asked.

"Yes. I asked Barlow. They interviewed him in his room yesterday. I don't know what all that flight behavior was about yesterday, but he appeared to be fine when they talked to him. He had nothing to offer and reported that he didn't know either one of them."

"That's a lie," she said, astonished.

"I know."

"You told them?"

"They knew."

Sarah sighed. "I agree with your earlier statement."

"What was that?" he asked, hoping she was beginning to agree that the integrity of Jeffrey Worme was in question.

"We need to get off this ship and clear our heads!"

"Great! What shall we do?" he asked.

"I feel like walking for hours on the beach along the water's edge," she said, stretching her arms above her head and yawning. "But let's save that until tomorrow and do nothing but that when we get to St. Thomas."

"Excellent plan! So how about today?" he asked.

"I feel like doing something that doesn't involve any planning or decisions on our part. How about we sign up for the city tour? They'll take us around in a bus to see what they want us to see, and they'll bring us back when they're good and ready. No decisions! How about it?"

"That sounds perfect. Shall we invite Sophie to join us?"

"I'll go ask her," Sarah said. "She might have plans with Jeffrey." She hesitated and added, "But I hope not."

Chapter 23

Charles and Sarah's last day in San Juan wasn't as relaxing as Sarah had hoped, but at least someone else made all the sightseeing decisions for them. Jeffrey still hadn't been heard from, and Sophie, feeling dejected, agreed to go with them. "He promised me a whole day of site seeing in San Juan, but I guess he has forgotten about me in all the excitement."

"I'm glad you're coming with us," Charles said, giving her arm a gentle squeeze. "This bus tour promises to show us the whole city." Once they boarded, Sophie sat immediately in front of Charles and Sarah, spreading out in hopes of keeping the entire seat to herself. When the driver started up, she turned in the seat so she could put her legs up and rest her ankle.

"Does it still hurt?" Charles asked.

"Only when I laugh," she responded without cracking a smile.

The tour bus traveled slowly through Old San Juan, and the driver pointed out the restored buildings from the sixteenth- and seventeenth-century Spanish colonial period. Colorful adobe buildings crowded the cobblestone streets with just enough space for a vehicle and a narrow pedestrian walkway. Other streets opened onto cobblestone squares with street vendors, sidewalk cafés, and statues reflecting the vast history of the area. "I'm glad we had a chance to walk through this area yesterday," Sarah said. "Viewing it from the bus doesn't do it justice."

From there, the bus headed for the coastline, where the white beach and emerald-green waters met the rocky peninsula that rose high above the sea. This was home to a historic fortress that defended the island against invaders during the seventeenth and eighteenth century. "I read about this," Charles said. "I'd like to come back if there's time this afternoon and take a tour. I understand it has tunnels and dungeons."

"Guy stuff," Sarah mouthed to Sophie, who nodded in agreement.

They crossed the bridge into San Juan proper and pulled up in front of the art museum. "We're going to stop here for an hour so you folks can explore the museum and the shops in the immediate neighborhood." After much persuasion, Sophie agreed to let Charles push her in a wheelchair so they could enjoy the museum without hurting her ankle. From there, the bus drove through the downtown area where Sarah and Charles had dinner the previous night. The driver pointed out historic and scenic sites, explaining the history as well as an occasional anecdote. They drove through parks and past churches, statues, theaters, and shopping areas. The driver would point out places that he recommended for those who were going to be on the island for a few days.

On their way back toward the ship, the bus stopped in Old San Juan so the passengers who wanted to could get out and see the 500-year-old gate, which was the original entrance to Old San Juan. He explained that just beyond the gate was home to San Juan's stray cat population.

"I wish we were going to have several more days here," Sarah commented as the bus approached the ship. "There's so much to see."

"I'm going to grab a cab and go back to the fortress," Charles announced as he walked the women up the gangplank. "Do you want to go with me?" he asked Sarah, knowing Sophie wasn't able to do that much walking.

"I talked to Stephanie this morning after breakfast. She's going to offer a few of the classes this afternoon for people who stayed behind. I think I would rather do that. I was so looking forward to the quilting aspect of the trip, and so far I haven't done much."

"I think I'm going to go rest for awhile," Sophie said. "Then I'm going to go find the elusive Mr. Worme and demand some answers." Sarah started to object but changed her mind. She headed for her room to freshen up and then to the Jupiter deck to see what classes were being held.

She immediately spotted the woman who was making the Sunbonnet Sue baby quilt. She had all her blocks made and was cutting out her sashing and borders. Stephanie walked into the classroom just then, and Sarah asked about the Sunbonnet Sue kits. Stephanie laughed, saying "I brought ten extra kits! Everyone always wants to do that quilt once they see it." Sarah pulled out her Sea Card to pay for the kit, but before she could hand it to her, Stephanie asked if she would like to trade her throw kit for the quilt kit.

"No, but thank you. I looked at the instructions in the throw kit, and I think I can do that one on my own when I get home. If I have problems, I'm sure someone at the quilt shop will help me. I want to start the Sunbonnet Sue while I'm on the ship and have you to help me," she said, smiling at Stephanie and feeling really fortunate to have access to someone so talented.

"Your appliqué stitch is good, Sarah. You'll have a few of these blocks done in no time. What other classes do you have?"

"Well, I signed up for the tote bag with the tropical birds. I really love the fabric but I've never made a bag," she added hesitantly.

"You can do that in an afternoon! It's a very simple pattern. Anything else?"

"Paper piecing."

"Perfect! You'll love that class, and Mary Kate is an excellent instructor. You'll learn a lot and have fun. I'll help you get started on your Sunbonnet Sue today. You can get one or two cut out and start your appliqué while I'm here to answer questions. Then you can work on the rest of them in your free time."

"I'd really love to finish everything and not go home with unfinished projects."

"You finished your wallhanging, and there's nothing to finish with the machine quilting class—just lots of practice. You can easily finish the other two projects during the time we have left, but the Sunbonnet Sue will take some time. There are many little pieces to be appliquéd: the dress, the apron, three hat pieces, the sleeve, the hand, and the shoe. There are also a couple of optional pieces, but you might not want to add those until you are more proficient."

"But I won't be able to finish it?" Sarah asked, looking disappointed.

"Just take your time. Appliqué should be relaxing and not rushed. Do some here where you can get help, and you'll be able to finish them at home," Stephanie said with a smile. As she walked away, she added, "Let me know if you have any questions."

Sarah spent the rest of the afternoon and into the evening concentrating on her adorable Sunbonnet Sue blocks. The fabrics in the kit were 1930s reproduction fabrics that made her think of the quilt on her grandmother's bed. Around 8:00 that evening, Charles stuck his head in the classroom. Sarah was the only person remaining. She jumped when he walked in. "What time is it?" she asked, amazed to see the sun low in the sky.

"Dinner time," he responded. She realized she was very hungry but had become lost in the comforting rhythm of hand stitching. She hadn't thought about Elwood or Matilda for many hours, and it had been a relief to just relax.

"I need to run by the room to leave my quilting bag and see if Sophie had dinner. Where do you want to go?"

"Let's keep it simple tonight. I wore myself out at the fortress. Those guys must have been in really good shape back then!"

"Those guys back then were probably half your age, old fellow," Sarah said with a chuckle.

Sophie joined them, and after a light dinner at one of the small cafés, all three retired to their rooms. Sophie said she hadn't been able to locate Jeffrey. He didn't answer his phone or return her messages.

"Maybe he's gone missing, too," Sarah said jokingly. She was immediately sorry.

Sophie looked at her with apprehension. "Do you think …?"

"No." Charles quickly assured her. "He's fine. I checked with Agent Barlow just before dinner. The FBI met with him this afternoon. He hasn't received a shore pass yet."

"Why?" Sophie asked, looking astonished. "Why would they want to keep him here?"

Charles looked at Sarah and she nodded. "It's time," she said, looking regretful. She hadn't wanted to share their concerns with Sophie, but she was beginning to think Sophie needed to know about their suspicions. Turning to Sophie, she said, "Sit down. We need to talk to you."

Chapter 24

That night the ship pulled away from San Juan and slowly traveled south to St. Thomas. The next morning the ship was docked in a breathtaking bay, with the tropical city of Charlotte Amalie wrapped around it. Charles had met with the purser to find out about the beaches. The purser recommended a white sandy beach on Magens Bay, which was on the opposite side of the island but only a fifteen-minute trip by cab.

After breakfast, Sarah and Charles layered shorts and tee-shirts over their bathing suits; packed up a bag with towels, lotion, and all the beach essentials they could think of; and headed down the gangplank. Charles was carrying a picnic basket in one hand (which their steward had arranged for) and the bag of essentials in the other.

Just like in San Juan, they were greeted at the end of the gangplank by a long line of eager taxi drivers. Another harrowing ride got them to a point overlooking Magens Bay in less than ten minutes.

As they got out of the cab, Charles asked, "What's the best way to get down to the beach?"

"Do you like to hike?" the cabbie asked.

"Sure. What do you have in mind?"

"Hop back in." On the short ride on up the hill, the driver told them about the Discovery Nature Trail, which winds a mile or so down to the beach. They were both excited about taking the trail, and the driver, Alfredo, agreed to meet them at the top of the trail at 4:00 in the afternoon to return them to the ship. Sarah slipped their tote bag over her shoulder and Charles picked up the picnic basket. He started to reach for the tote bag as well, but she made it obvious with a look that he should let her carry it.

Walking was treacherous until they got used to the bark-filled steps that carried them down toward the beach. At first they found themselves winding through a moist tropical forest. As the path continued to wind downward toward the beach, they came to a boardwalk, which led them through low growing trees with roots above the ground. "Mangroves, I think they're called," Charles said just as they arrived at a sign that confirmed the name and said they grew near the water.

"We must be close," Sarah said, beginning to get winded from walking in the extreme heat. Turning a corner at the end of the trail, they found themselves on a beautiful beach. White sand stretched in both directions in the shape of a horseshoe and wrapped around a calm turquoise bay. Sailboats drifted sleepily at a distance.

"Magens Bay!" Charles announced with a sweep of his arm. It wasn't totally secluded, but the nearest people were at least a quarter mile away. They could see a bayside hotel far up the beach, and most of the people were congregated near there. "We'll walk in the other direction," Charles said, indicating the opposite arm of the bay where it became more desolate.

The couple spent the day exactly as Sarah had imagined. They walked for miles up and down the beach. When they got too warm, they swam in the clear waters among brightly colored fish swooping around them playfully. "It's just like swimming in a tropical fish tank!" Sarah announced excitedly.

In the early afternoon, after a delicious lunch of sandwiches and tropical fruits, they spread their towels out under a grove of palm trees and lay down side by side. Charles took her hand and squeezed gently.

"Let's stay right here forever," she responded wistfully. He turned and kissed her gently.

They fell asleep and Sarah awoke later with a start. "What time is it?" she asked the sleeping man beside her.

"What? Oh my! It's 3:30 already! We'd better get moving." They grabbed their things and headed back up the nature trail. Going up was much more difficult than going down. When they reached the top, they were both panting.

Alfredo was waiting at the top and laughed when he saw them. "I should have warned you about the trip up," he said jokingly. When they got into the cab, Alfredo passed two bottles of ice-cold water back to them. Making a chilling U-turn, he headed back to the ship at breakneck speed.

"You two look terrible! What happened to you out there?" Sophie was relaxed and looking refreshed in her white gauze dress and island jewelry. Sarah and Charles were tired, sunburned, covered with sand, and poorly coiffed. "Not a pretty sight," Sophie added, shaking her head and returning to her room.

"See you later," Charles said as he headed for his room.

"Much later," Sarah responded. "Much *much* later!"

Once she had her shower and put her wet, sandy clothes in the laundry bag for the steward, she stretched out on the bed and put in a call to Matilda's room.

"Hello," Matilda answered.

"Matilda, it's Sarah. I was wondering how you are doing today."

"I'm better."

"Any word yet?"

"No. The coast guard notified the captain that there was no sign of Elwood in the waters they searched. Surely they didn't really expect to find him," Matilda added sarcastically.

"So what's next? Do you know?" Sarah asked.

"They're saying he is *presumed dead.* I'm not sure what that means. I contacted my insurance agent but didn't get anywhere. They are going to talk to the ship's captain. I think they are going to give me trouble ..."

Matilda went on talking about the insurance and the investigation but Sarah wasn't listening. *What's wrong with this woman? She just lost her husband!* Sarah thought back about the months following her own husband's death. She didn't even want to get out of bed, much less talk to an insurance agent.

"Are you flying home?" Sarah asked. She knew the cruise line had offered to fly Matilda from St. Thomas back to Baltimore.

"Absolutely not! I paid for this trip. I'm going to take it. Besides, I'm signed up for several more classes ..."

Again, Sarah was dumbfounded by what she was hearing. "Oh, there's someone at my door, Matilda. I'll talk to you later." Sarah was sorry about the white lie, but she didn't know what to say to this woman; she wanted to talk to Charles. She slipped her robe on and tapped on their adjoining door.

"Yes?" he said.

"Open up, please. I need to talk."

"Hold on, I'm not dressed."

"Neither am I. Just hurry please."

When he opened the door, he had pulled on his jeans and a top that she assumed was his pajama top. "Cute," she said teasingly.

"You, too." He looked at her inquisitively. He almost said, "What's up?" but she had told him once how much she disliked that greeting. "It's such a put-off," she had said. He didn't say anything and waited for her to speak.

"Come on in," she said as she pulled a coke from the cooler and split it between them. They sat down on the love seat and she told him about her conversation with Matilda. "What do you think?"

"Sarah, I don't know what to think. I've investigated many cases, and the families of the victims have a whole range of reactions from grief to denial. Sometimes they are just relieved. At first, I thought she was in shock. I don't think that anymore. I just don't think she cares one way or the other. That doesn't mean she killed him. It doesn't mean she *didn't* kill him."

Sarah sat quietly and listened. "What should I do?"

"You should stay out of it. She might be dangerous. She might be mentally ill. But whatever she is, I don't want you in any danger." They didn't say much more about it. He was surprised Matilda didn't want to be flown home.

They finally decided to let the topic go for the time being. Charles was planning to talk with the captain the next day and see what progress had been made in the investigation.

There was a tap at the other adjoining door, and Sophie stepped in. "You two don't look much better. Cleaner, but not much better. Are you folks going to dinner tonight?"

"We are all going," Charles responded. "Did you forget I have tickets for the three of us at the dinner theater tonight? It starts at 8:00."

"Am I dressed okay?" Sophie asked reluctantly.

"Yes! You're dressed just fine. It's dressy casual, which means your pretty white dress and jewelry are just right." Sophie looked hesitant, as if she were about to say something.

"What is it, Sophie? Don't you want to go?"

"Yes. Maybe. I was just hoping ..." Sophie stopped mid-sentence. Sarah looked at Charles, and they both knew how the sentence was going to end.

"Were you hoping to hear from Jeffrey?" Sarah asked gently.

"Yes. But I know that's silly. It's just that ..." Again, she stopped talking. She stood up abruptly and reached for her cane. "I'm going to take a walk. I'll meet you at the theater at 8:00." And she hobbled out the door.

"She is probably hoping to run into him. I think our suspicions really upset her," Charles said. "I'm going to go get dressed. Let's call in for some appetizers and wine, and we'll have a little pre-theater snack. All that fresh air and exercise has me starving!" Sarah smiled her agreement and said for him to come back in a half hour ready to party. Actually, she was feeling like a nice long nap, but with the play in just two hours, there wasn't time. *I'll have plenty of time to rest back in Middletown*, she assured herself.

Chapter 25

Sarah looked back on her previous day of relaxation and realized how important it was to set life aside now and then and just *play*. The day at the beach and the evening of good food and entertainment had rejuvenated her and helped her get some perspective on the whole situation with Matilda. Sarah was going to spend time with her and give her an opportunity to talk, but she wasn't going to attempt to figure out what part she may have played in Elwood's disappearance. She would leave that to the law enforcement folks. In the meantime, she knew Matilda needed a friend.

After breakfast, she took out her project tote and called Matilda. Matilda answered on the first ring, and Sarah asked her about her plans. "I have a class today," she said. Sarah ignored the fact that she hadn't even mentioned Elwood. Sarah didn't mention him either.

"So do I," Sarah responded. "I'm in the paper-piecing class. What are you taking?"

"I'm starting a wallhanging that's called a *color wash*. It almost looks like a French impressionist painting."

"Are you doing that one by hand, too?"

"I'm thinking about giving machine piecing a try. You just sew long strips together and cut them apart. It would probably be easiest on a machine."

Sarah was amazed at how calmly Matilda talked about her plans. She didn't seem to be thinking about Elwood at all. Of course, she knew that a person's public face could be very deceiving. Sarah offered to give her a quick lesson on the machine and get it threaded for her. They arranged to meet in the classroom an hour before class time.

Once Matilda got accustomed to the machine, she had no problem sewing a straight line. That was all she was going to need for her project. Matilda pulled out her kit and Sarah saw that the strips were precut, which was going to make it easy. Sarah showed her how to make sure she had a consistent quarter-inch seam.

As they were finishing up, other members of the class began coming in, so Sarah headed for her own classroom. She had no idea what she would be doing but was eager to learn about paper piecing. *Forty-five minutes together and not a word about Elwood*, she marveled.

Sarah's instructor, Mary Kate, was displaying the wallhanging and one of the blocks when Sarah entered the classroom. The wallhanging looked like a sunburst in shades of gold and yellow batiks. Sarah looked closely and marveled at how perfect the points were. Not a single point had been lost in the seams. She had read in the brochure that precision was the benefit of paper piecing.

When the rest of the class arrived, Mary Kate introduced herself and talked about the basic concepts of paper piecing. She said it was an outgrowth of the old-fashioned foundation piecing that was done with newspaper or old fabric.

Mary Kate passed out paper versions of the quilt block. She explained how to use it to line up two pieces of fabric behind it and then sew, following the lines on the paper in order to make a perfect block. It sounded confusing at first, but once Sarah saw Mary Kate do a block, it became clear.

Within the first three hours, Sarah had completed nine perfect blocks that were ready to trim and sew together. Each block had thin pointed triangles in shades of yellow and gold that represented the rays of the sun. Sarah stood back and marveled at the modernistic, brightly colored wallhanging she had created. "It's breathtaking," she muttered to herself.

Sarah took a short lunch break on the deck and quietly worked on her Sunbonnet Sue quilt as she enjoyed the gentle breeze and warm sunshine. She had picked up a sandwich and a soda at a nearby café but chose to go off by herself for some much-needed alone time. Looking out over the water, she felt totally at peace.

During the last two hours of the class, Sarah cut the accent strips for her wallhanging. She easily assembled it, and her wallhanging was ready for the quilter when she returned home. She wanted to hang it in her living room and was reluctant to do her own quilting just yet. She wanted the quilting to be as perfect as the quilt top.

By 4:00 in the afternoon, Sarah was finished with her wallhanging and headed back to her room. On her way, she stuck her head in Matilda's class and saw that she was making incredible progress on her color wash. Matilda said she was going to continue sewing into the evening. Sarah wondered if she had had any contact with the FBI agents who remained onboard or with the captain, but she chose not to bring up the subject. *If she can pretend it never happened, so can I.*

* * * * *

Charles, Captain Wanamaker, and Agent Barlow sat around the small conference-room table in the captain's office. The captain had requested that Charles join them to discuss a development. A young man had been caught rummaging through the Knowles stateroom while Matilda was out.

He was detained by Agent Barlow and interrogated. He had a thick accent and didn't seem to understand many of their questions. He claimed to be from Armenia but had been living in the United States for the past ten years. When asked about the break-in, he claimed that he didn't understand the question. Later he said he thought he was in his own room.

Agent Barlow went on to say, "We have him confined to his room right now. We aren't sure what to do with him. We only have him on breaking and entering, but there must be more to it. He doesn't understand much English, considering that he lives in the United States," Barlow added.

"Do you have a picture of the guy?" The agent pulled a picture out of his file folder and passed it to Charles.

"I know this guy." Charles commented. "He understands English just fine."

Charles told the captain and agent Barlow about this man talking to him in the auditorium while he was waiting for his interview. The man had been intrusive, Charles felt, and he was very interested in Sarah and her connection to Matilda. "It hadn't occurred to me to be concerned about the guy at the time, but now that I see his picture, I'm glad he's being confined. What do you think he was up to?" Charles asked, handing the picture back to Barlow.

"We were hoping you might have some idea. Do you know what this Elwood character did for a living?"

"No. I have no idea," Charles responded. "He only told me *this and that*, which was suspicious at the time. What does his wife say?"

"She's vague about it, too. She's claiming she doesn't know where his money comes from. She said he used to work for an insurance company but was laid off a few years ago."

"And this man? What's his line?"

"He claims to be unemployed."

"Unemployed and on a cruise? That's strange. What's his name?"

"Sargsyan. Alex Sargsyan."

Charles sighed deeply and shook his head. "This is becoming *curiouser and curiouser*!"

"Spoken like a man with a grandchild!" Captain Wanamaker laughed.

"Actually, no. I was sitting on the Sky deck by the kiddie pool, and a little girl was reading *Alice in Wonderland* to her little brother. You don't see that much anymore. Not one kid in that family had an electronic gadget."

After a short silence, Barlow said, "Back to Sargsyan. Any ideas what he's after?"

"How about something incriminating? Has the room been searched?" Charles asked.

"Thoroughly after Knowles went missing. But we weren't thinking in terms of an Armenian expatriate."

"I can't think how that might change the search," Charles said. "You need for this guy to talk." Turning to Barlow, he asked, "Do you folks have any resources to get him talking?"

"Nothing legal," Barlow responded, and the group sat, silently absorbing that piece of information.

The three men didn't resolve their dilemma, but Barlow decided to question Sargsyan one more time to see if there was any variation in his story. Charles returned to his room and found Sarah just coming back from class.

"How did it go?" he asked. She showed him the wallhanging, and even he, a person with no knowledge of quilting, was impressed with the precision.

"Tell me about your day."

Charles told her about his meeting with the captain and Barlow. She was surprised to hear about the intruder, especially since Matilda hadn't mentioned it that morning. They stretched out on deck chairs on Sarah's balcony. Charles had ordered a pitcher of lemonade, which sat between them, along with some small pastries.

"Have you figured out who killed Elwood?" she asked him in a less-than-serious tone. She knew he hadn't.

"… If he *was* even killed," Charles responded.

"What else could have happened? He's not on the ship."

"Maybe he fell off," Charles suggested, sipping his lemonade.

"During the storm?"

"Um hum."

"Maybe he jumped off," Sarah responded.

"Maybe he was pushed off …" Charles said.

"By whom?" she asked.

"By Jeffrey, maybe," Charles responded.

"Or by Matilda," she countered.

"Or maybe this newcomer, Alex Sargsyan ..." Charles suggested.

"Or maybe, as you said in the beginning, he simply fell off the ship."

"Hmm. Not likely," Charles responded thoughtfully. "Not likely."

"Okay. Then maybe we should be looking at the possible motives if we are considering murder. Starting with Matilda, why would Matilda want him dead?"

"She told you herself," Charles responded. "For the insurance."

"She told me that?"

"Sure. She has already tried to file a claim."

"Oh. Okay, why would Jeffrey want to kill him?" she asked. "To get Matilda for himself?"

"Hmm," he responded pensively. Raising his eyebrows and one finger as if he had an idea, Charles said, "Remember when I found Jeffrey and Elwood in the corridor arguing? Well, we all assumed they were fighting because of Jeffrey flirting with Matilda. Maybe, just maybe," he added speculatively, "they're in some sort of business together."

"Maybe something illegal, even," Sarah added.

"Maybe it even involves this Sargsyan guy." Charles contemplated this idea for a moment and then added, "And maybe Jeffrey's mysterious trip to San Juan is related in some way? Or maybe ..."

Sarah interrupted, saying, "... or maybe Elwood just fell off the boat."

Charles looked deflated. "You are ruining my fun," he complained.

Chapter 26

"We only have a couple more days at sea," Sarah said as she and Charles walked along the deck and looked out over the ocean early one morning. "I'll miss this."

"I'll miss spending so much time with you. This has been a dream come true for me." He stopped, gazed into her eyes, and saw a tiny tear form and slide down her right cheek. "What is it, sweetheart?" he asked, becoming worried and still incapable of reading her expressions.

"I'll miss you, too," she said simply.

"I think when we get home and get grounded in our *real life*, we need to have a serious talk about our future." He was nervous about saying this. She had balked in the past when he even suggested that they needed to talk about where their relationship was headed.

"I think so too, Charles. I think so too." She laid her head against his chest, and he was sure she could hear his heart pounding. *Did she really say she thinks so too?* He wrapped his arms around her, and they stood that way for several minutes.

"But first," she added, "We have to get away from this romantic fantasy world!"

He felt his heart sink. *Was she going to change her mind when they got home?*

"But we'll still talk, right?" he asked reluctantly.

"You bet we will," she responded, tapping him gently with her fist. "You can't get out of it now." He felt his heart smile.

They headed toward the dining room and the bountiful breakfast buffet. Looking across the room, Sarah thought she saw Jeffrey sitting with a woman. The way they were sitting, Jeffrey was blocking her view, but it looked as if it might be Sophie. *It can't be*, she thought.

As Sarah was sitting down, she got a better view, and it was definitely Sophie. At that moment, Jeffrey leaned across the table and kissed her. "Did you see that?" she asked Charles, who was behind her holding her chair.

"I sure did," he responded.

"She's been calling him *The Worm* since we left St. Thomas. What do you suppose happened?"

"I think she will tell us when she is ready," Charles responded, sitting down and picking up his napkin.

"But ..."

"Honey, she's a big girl. Let her have her fun. We'll all be back home in a couple of days."

"I just worry about her," Sarah sighed.

As they were walking to the buffet, Sophie and Jeffrey caught up with them. Sophie was flushed and looking excited. Jeffrey looked at Charles a little sheepishly and said, "I haven't seen you folks for a few days. Lots of excitement around here."

"Sure has been," Charles responded. "I understand you didn't know the couple involved."

"Oh. Well … I didn't know the wife. I think I met the husband once. Real sad thing about him. I heard he threw himself in the ocean." He frowned and, shaking his head in amazement, added, "Terrible way to go. Terrible."

"Um," Charles grunted without looking at him. "If that's what really happened."

Jeffrey appeared flustered and moved to the end of the buffet to get a plate. Sophie stayed with Charles and Sarah. "Let him off the hook, guys. He's okay."

"Just take care of yourself," Sarah said. "He could be dangerous."

"He's a pussy cat!" she responded with a chuckle and hobbled over to his side.

Charles and Sarah returned to their table and ate in silence, both deep in thought. Sarah was preoccupied with concern for Sophie and Charles was preoccupied with the mental puzzle. Charles had been trying to remove himself from the case. With the FBI on it, it was really none of his concern, but there were so many aspects that bothered him. He couldn't resist trying to fit the incongruous pieces together. *Something is very wrong*, he thought. *Very wrong.*

Sarah spent most of the day in the quilting room. She worked on her Sunbonnet Sue blocks until it was time for her tote bag class, which turned out to be just as easy as Stephanie had promised. The fabric was brightly colored and covered with tropical birds and island scenes.

When she finished the tote, she took it to show Matilda who was working on her color wash in the next classroom. "I just can't seem to concentrate today," Matilda said after admiring the bag.

"It's no wonder," Sarah responded. "Look at what you've been through!" It was the first time she had made any reference to Elwood's disappearance, and she hoped Matilda might say something about it, but she didn't. Sarah sat down next to her and pulled out her Sunbonnet Sue block. They worked quietly together for an hour or so.

In the late afternoon, they both stood up to leave. "Are you going to the banquet tonight?" Sarah asked Matilda.

"Oh, I don't know. I don't really think …"

"Matilda, come with us. Please. We'll all sit together and have a few drinks and just relax. It's our last night. Your next few days are going to be very stressful. How about one night of relaxation?"

Matilda smiled for the first time in days. She had been holding her face tight and drawn. "Do you think your friends will mind?"

"Absolutely not! They will be happy to have you there." She knew this wasn't entirely true, but she thought it would give Charles a chance to talk with her.

"You've invited a killer to have dinner with us?" Sophie asked, looking astonished.

"Sophie, we don't know that she did anything. And she certainly isn't going to kill any of us! This will give Charles a chance to figure out how he feels about her possible involvement."

"Well, he's going to be one busy fellow tonight. I'm bringing Jeffrey. Is Charles going to be interrogating him as well?"

Hiding her surprise that Jeffrey would be there, she responded cheerfully, "Charles won't interrogate anyone. It will be fine." She didn't believe that, of course. They were going to be dining with two of the principle suspects in a possible murder. She wondered what Charles would think of this. She wondered if she had made a mistake.

Reassuring herself as well as Sophie, Sarah said, "Remember, there may have been no murder at all. It could have been a simple accident." Opening the connecting door, she went into her room to get ready for the evening.

"You're right," Sophie called after her. "He probably just fell off the boat."

"Ship," Sarah corrected as she closed the door.

Chapter 27

The final banquet was a formal affair. Sarah was dressed in a long silk dress in a gentle shade of teal. The dress was sleeveless and cut a little lower than she was accustomed. She added a bolero-style jacket and felt less exposed. Walking into the banquet room, however, she realized her gown was much more modest than most, and she vowed to remove the jacket later in the evening.

Charles was dressed black tie with a white jacket. Sarah thought he looked incredibly handsome. She didn't see a single younger man that could hold a candle to her attractive date. As usual, a blond curl slipped down on his forehead as he bent to pull her chair out. It made her smile. "Are you laughing at me?" he asked jokingly.

"I'm just very happy," she responded. "Will you help me with my jacket?"

"Whew," he said, looking at her. "You are by far the most beautiful woman in the room."

Sarah laughed and responded, "I am by far one of the *oldest* women in the room!" Of course that was far from true. It was hard for her to accept compliments. She was embarrassed, and she quickly changed the subject. "Have you seen Sophie and Jeffrey yet?"

At that moment, she saw Matilda hesitantly approaching the door. Sarah turned to Charles and asked that he go escort her to their table. She saw Matilda turn as if to leave. "Hurry," she said to Charles. He caught up with Matilda just as she was starting to walk away. They stood and talked for a few moments, and then he took her arm and led her to the table. Matilda was dressed in a long black dress with a loose jacket. Being very thin, the outfit hung on her, appearing to be too big.

"You look pretty," Sarah greeted, hoping to help her relax.

"Thank you. The formal dress I brought is red. It didn't seem appropriate under the circumstances. I found this at the onboard shop, but it's a little big."

Charles seated her next to Sarah. The next two seats were being saved for Sophie and Jeffrey. Charles placed their drink order after confirming what the women wanted. As the drinks were being served, Sophie and Jeffrey arrived. Matilda's back was to the door, so she didn't see them, and Jeffrey obviously didn't recognize her from the back.

Jeffrey approached the table a bit more boisterous than usual, greeting Charles with an energetic handshake and putting his hand on Sarah's shoulder as he said hello. He looked at the woman next to Sarah just as she looked up. They both froze.

Matilda recovered first, saying, "We meet again, Mr. Worme."

"Again?" he responded, looking embarrassed and avoiding Charles' eyes. "I don't believe I've had the pleasure."

To relieve the tension, Charles stood, introduced everyone, and directed the newcomers to their seats. "What's your drink?" he asked cordially. Matilda appeared to be steaming with anger.

"Are you okay?" Sarah asked.

"Yes. It's just been a difficult few days." *Difficult? I should think so!* Sarah thought but didn't say. There was tension at the table for the first hour. Matilda and Jeffrey never spoke directly to one another. Matilda was very cool toward Sophie and only spoke to Sarah and Charles when they addressed her. Sarah was beginning to think it was a mistake to invite Matilda to join them. Fortunately, Sophie got started telling her raucous stories, which began to relieve the tension. Even Matilda laughed at one point. Charles ordered another round of drinks for everyone, and Sarah began to think the group would make it through dinner.

The table was set for a party of six, which left an empty seat between Charles and Sophie. At one point, just before the appetizers were served, Matilda and Sarah excused themselves and headed for the ladies' room. Sophie grabbed her cane and hobbled along with them.

"That's one tense lady," Jeffrey said to Charles, nodding toward Matilda.

"Um."

When they returned, Matilda headed for the empty seat between Charles and Sophie. She was now facing Jeffrey instead of sitting next to him.

"I think you would've enjoyed show-and-tell this afternoon. It was really inspiring," Sarah said, leaning across Charles to see if she could engage Matilda in conversation.

"I had some things to take care of," Matilda responded, glancing at Jeffrey who immediately looked away.

Sarah continued. "Each class got up as a group and displayed their projects. It was really interesting to see how the same pattern looked after being made up in different fabrics and colors." Matilda gave her a weak smile, but Sarah went on. "Everyone laughed, though, when the three tote bag classes stood up together. We had thirty-two women standing in a long line, all with the same bag on their shoulders. That was a lot of parrots!" Matilda gave another weak smile.

Sarah was finding it impossible to get a conversation going with Matilda, so she sat back and stopped trying. She had no idea what Matilda might be feeling under the circumstances, but she wasn't going to let it ruin her evening.

Sarah noticed that Matilda exchanged a few strained pleasantries with Sophie, but there definitely seemed to be an odd tension between Matilda and Jeffrey. *Could she be jealous of Sophie?* Sarah wondered. *And if so, why?* She was beginning to agree with Charles that there must be something connecting all these people: Elwood, Jeffrey, Matilda, and maybe even the Armenian guy.

Much of the tension dissipated once dinner arrived. By this time, each person had each had at least one cocktail. The group was loosening up and eager to see what would be served at this gala affair. To begin, each person was brought a jumbo shrimp cocktail and a cup of lobster bisque, followed by a baby-leaf spinach and mushroom salad. For their main course, Sarah and Matilda had both ordered the *duck à l'orange*, and the men had ordered lobster. Sophie had ordered a filet mignon, which she later said was done to perfection. The accompaniments were meticulously prepared and tastefully presented.

By the time dessert was offered, the group had lingered for over two hours, sipping wine and enjoying the elegant meal. They laughed when the dessert cart was presented, everyone saying they couldn't eat another bite. However, they were all able to enjoy the shared caramel pecan praline, the chocolate truffle, and the rich, creamy tiramisu, which they passed back and forth across the table.

During the evening the captain circulated, visiting each table and encouraging passengers to return. At the next table, Sarah overheard him apologize for the inconveniences they had experienced in San Juan, but he didn't mention it at their table—probably out of deference to Matilda. Earlier that day, everyone had received a personalized certificate awarding a $500 discount on a future trip because of the delays in San Juan.

About that time, a propitious event occurred that would lead to unexpected results. A photographer who was offering everyone the opportunity to be photographed in their formal attire stopped at their table. Charles had brought his own camera and had been snapping his own pictures, primarily of Sarah, but when the photographer came by their table, he suggested they have a group picture taken. Sarah moved to Jeffrey's chair, which put the three women sitting in a row on one side of the table. The two men stood behind them, and the photographer took several shots. Charles reviewed the shots, chose one, and pulled out his Sea Card. He ordered five copies to be delivered to his room.

After the photographer left, they noticed several other tables were beginning to disperse. "Sarah, would you mind if I take just a couple more pictures of you here at the table?"

"You're being silly! What are you going to do with all these pictures of me?" she asked teasingly. Nevertheless, she touched her hair to make sure it was properly arranged and she smiled. Charles snapped several pictures and was about to take another one when she said, "Okay! That's it! No more pictures."

Charles and Jeffrey shook hands and Sarah hugged Matilda. "May we walk you to your room?" she asked.

"I'll be fine," she responded. "I'm going to start packing. I have Elwood's clothes to pack up." For just a moment, she looked out toward the ocean, and Sarah thought she saw a flicker of the pain this woman must be feeling.

"Call me if you need me," Sarah offered.

Jeffrey put his arm around Sophie, guiding her to the door. Matilda shot him a murderous glare.

So much for the flicker of pain, Sarah thought, shaking her head.

Chapter 28

The steward had just delivered the pictures from the evening before, and Charles stared at the group, trying to identify what was nagging at him. He had taken a few pictures every day with his own camera but hadn't downloaded them yet. He decided to go ahead and do that now.

As he watched the pictures appear on his laptop, one face grabbed his attention. *Who was that?* he wondered. When they were all downloaded, he scanned back to the picture. It had been taken several days earlier on the Sun deck.

Something niggled at him. He went back to the photographer's picture from the banquet, but that one didn't bother him as much. He felt like the answer was just out of his reach.

Charles clicked over to his email program and sent a quick note to Matt, his lieutenant. He asked Matt to send him a DMV picture of Elwood Knowles. Within an hour, the picture of Knowles arrived. Charles had to sit down when he opened the file.

What? Charles sat there dazed.

Once he got himself together, Charles whipped out a response to Matt. Within an hour, the steward came to the door, saying that he was wanted immediately in the captain's quarters. He was annoyed by the interruption, but he sighed and followed the steward past the bridge and to the captain's quarters. Agent Barlow was with the captain when he arrived.

The captain explained that he had received a call from Lieutenant Matthew Stokely. He went on to tell Charles what the lieutenant had discussed with him and then instructed Charles to call Stokely immediately.

Charles and Stokely talked extensively on speaker, and Barlow interjected questions along the way. Once their plans were finalized, Charles thanked the captain and they shook hands. He knew he couldn't tell Sarah. He couldn't expect her to carry the burden of keeping this to herself. He hoped she would forgive him. Charles returned to his room, looking forward to opening his flask and pouring a long tall drink.

Chapter 29

The next morning, the group walked down the gangplank with mixed emotions. Sarah was sorry to see their vacation ending but was eager to get back to her routine and her dog. She knew she would miss being with Charles every day. Their time together aboard ship had brought them closer, and she was aware there was no turning back.

Sophie was smiling as she walked proudly down the plank, holding Jeffrey's arm. She had had a great time and hoped they could do this again one day. She knew Jeffrey wasn't going to be a part of her life beyond the cruise, but he had helped her open doors she thought were closed forever. She hadn't flirted for many years and even now blushed at the memory. It had been fun!

Charles was tense, waiting for the other shoe to drop.

Matilda looked apprehensive, and Sarah knew it must be difficult to leave the ship alone. *Matilda came on this cruise as a wife and is leaving as a widow.* Sarah put her arm around the frail woman's shoulder as they walked. Charles walked behind the group, as always, making sure everything was working as it should.

Halfway down the gangplank, the group moved to the side to allow two members of the ship's security team to pass them. Alex Sargsyan walked between the two men with his head hanging. Charles knew one of the security men and asked what was happening. "Theft," he replied. "He's been stealing jewelry from empty staterooms."

"Hmm."

As they approached the dock, two uniformed officers took possession of the humiliated Armenian.

The group resumed walking down the gangplank, Jeffrey and Sophie in the lead and Charles bringing up the rear.

Four uniformed police officers walked up the gangplank toward Jeffrey, two with their guns drawn. The officer in the lead grabbed Jeffrey's arm and with one swift movement, had him in handcuffs. Another officer did the same with Matilda. Sarah screamed, "What are you doing?"

"Elwood Knowles," the first officer said to Jeffrey. "You are under arrest for conspiracy to perform insurance fraud. You have the right to remain silent, if …"

Simultaneously, the second officer began reading Matilda her rights.

"Stop!" Sarah demanded. "You've got it all wrong! This isn't Elwood. This is Jeffrey Worme! Elwood Knowles is dead!" Confused by what was happening, she turned to Charles. "Tell them, Charles!"

"Lady, keep out of this," the officer ordered. Behind the police officers, Charles saw a team of FBI agents approaching.

Charles reached for his identification, and the officer pulled his gun. "Wait, please." Charles implored. "I'm reaching for my ID. I'm a retired cop, Charles Parker." He pulled out his identification and showed it to the officer.

"Oh. Okay, Parker. I was told to connect with you here." the officer replied. "We'll talk in a minute."

"What's going on?" Sarah cried, looking at Charles. "Tell them this is Jeffrey Worme, not Elwood Knowles. Tell them Elwood is dead!" She moved to his side and clung to his arm. "Straighten them out," she pleaded. "Why aren't you helping Jeffrey?"

"Sarah, honey," Charles responded, pointing at Jeffrey, "This *is* Elwood Knowles, also known as Jeffrey Worme. And this," he added, pointing to Matilda, "is Elwood's dear wife, Matilda Knowles. Together they were planning to rip off the cruise line and their own insurance company for millions of dollars."

Sarah looked at Matilda. Instead of the tense look she had become accustomed to, Sarah saw intense anger.

"Then who is dead?" Sarah asked, looking bewildered.

"No one, you fool!" Matilda snarled. "No one!" And she pulled off her cap of soft brown curls to reveal her thin gray hair.

"Elwood?" Sophie gasped, looking at Matilda, bewildered. "Jeffrey?" she said, looking from Matilda to Jeffrey. "I don't understand."

Jeffrey, as Sophie knew him, stood looking contrite with his arms handcuffed behind his back. He shrugged and said, "Sorry, Soph. You're a nice lady. I'm sorry if I've hurt you."

Matilda glared at her husband. "Sorry! *Sorry* is exactly what you are. You are one sorry excuse for a man. I should have left you home like I wanted to," she snarled. "I knew you would ruin this for me."

"For *you*?" Jeffrey, now Elwood, responded. "I thought this was for *us*." Matilda lunged toward her husband, but the officer stopped her by grabbing her handcuffed arm."

"Hey!" she grimaced angrily. "You're hurting me!"

"Let's go, folks. We can sort this out at the station."

"Is anyone going to tell me what's going on?" Sophie demanded, resuming her familiar confident stance.

Charles put his arm around her shoulder and gently said, "Let's all go to the station, and then we'll head back home. I'll explain the whole thing on the way." He reached for Sarah, whose eyes were still large with shock. "Come on, honey. Let's go."

Sitting in the back of the cab between Charles and Sarah, Sophie began to speak softly. "Matilda was Elwood? Jeffrey was Elwood? And no one is dead?"

"Yes," Charles said reassuringly. "Matilda was masquerading as Elwood. The Elwood we met never existed. That was simply Matilda in disguise. And her *real* husband, Elwood, was pretending to be a man named Jeffrey Worme."

"Appropriate choice of names," Sarah muttered to herself. "The worm!"

Everyone was quiet for a while, and then Sarah turned to Charles, "How did she do it?"

"She did it with a wig, tinted contacts, lots of theatrical makeup, and lifts when she was pretending to be Elwood. If you think about it, she didn't let us see much of him."

"Didn't they both have to check in with the purser when they boarded?" Sarah asked.

"The captain and I talked about that. He thinks Matilda came onboard as Elwood, changed, pulled the emergency alarm, and snuck off the ship in the confusion. Then she came back on and checked in as herself."

"We never saw them together," she said contemplatively. "We should have realized ..."

"Who would ever think of this?" he responded. "We noticed they never ate together but we never thought about the fact that they were never together any other time."

"But why? I don't understand why," Sophie said. "Why did they go to all that trouble?"

Charles responded, "So they could pretend Elwood was dead and file for the insurance benefits—several million dollars. They were probably planning to sue the cruise line, as well, for negligence and get another million or two."

"Why do you suppose Jeffrey, I mean Elwood, hung around Sophie like he did?" Sarah asked, still trying to fit all the pieces together.

Not waiting for Charles' response, Sophie sat tall and declared proudly, "Because I'm a beautiful person and men love me!"

Charles laughed, saying, "That's absolutely right. Also, he is a womanizer and is attracted to strong women."

"That's Sophie!" Sarah said. "A strong woman!"

"That's who I am," Sophie agreed, slipping on her big round purple glasses. "Beautiful and strong. Let's go home!"

PROJECT

SUNBURST

See full quilt on back cover.

While on a quilting cruise, Sarah admired the perfect points in this 24″ × 29½″ wallhanging. Paper piecing will give you the same stunning results.

MATERIALS

Assorted batik fabrics: 2½ yards total

Accent batik: ¼ yard *or* 6 rectangles, each 3¼″ × 8½″

Foundation paper, such as Carol Doak's Foundation Paper (by C&T Publishing): 9 pieces 8½″ × 11″

Backing: ⅞ yard

Binding: ⅓ yard

Batting: 28″ × 34″

Project Instructions

Seam allowances are ¼″.

PAPER PIECE THE BLOCKS

Tip ‖ Use a short stitch length throughout (15–20 per inch) to keep your stitches secure when removing the foundation paper.

1. Print the block pattern (page 212) on foundation paper. Trim to 8½″ × 8½″. Make 9.

2. Paper piece each block, adding the fabrics in the order shown on the pattern. Press after each addition. Refer to *Paper Pieced Modern* by Amy Garro (by C&T Publishing) for step-by-step instructions on paper piecing.

3. Make 9 blocks. Trim each to 8½″ × 8½″.

ASSEMBLE AND FINISH THE QUILT

1. Sew 3 blocks and 2 accent rectangles together to make a column. Press. Make 3 columns. *Note:* The orientation and placement of the blocks and accent rectangles differ for each column.

2. Sew the 3 columns together. Press.

3. Remove the foundation paper from the back of the blocks.

4. Layer the pieced top with the batting and backing. Quilt and bind as desired.

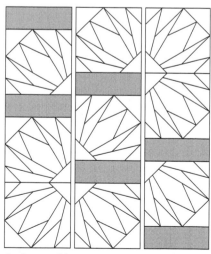

Quilt assembly

PROJECT

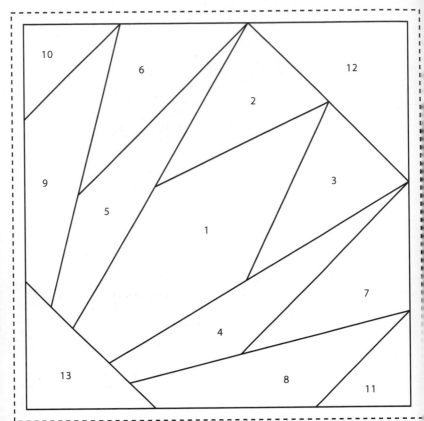

Block pattern: Enlarge 200%

Keep reading for a preview - ➔
of the next book in A Quilting Cozy series.

2nd edition includes instructions to make the featured quilt

Patchwork Connections

a quilting cozy

Carol Dean Jones

Preview of *Patchwork Connections*

Martha turned her headlights off and drove slowly past her house. The black car was parked across the street. There was no moon, but even in the dark of night, she recognized the car. It had been outside her house frequently over the past few weeks. It was sometimes in her office parking lot. Occasionally she would see it in her rearview mirror as she drove. She reported it to the police, but no laws had been broken. At least not yet.

She attempted to garner enough courage to stop and confront the driver, but fear held her back. As she passed the car, she could make out a shadowy figure and the red tip of a burning cigarette.

Martha turned left at the next corner and again into the alley behind her house. Trembling, she slipped out of the car and hurried into the house. She grabbed her phone to call the police but went to the window and, as always, the car was gone.

She hung up without dialing. Again.

* * * * *

"I can't possibly manage the shop while you're away, Ruth! I know nothing about running a quilt shop!" Sarah exclaimed.

"Sarah!" Ruth retorted. "You managed the largest grocery store in Middletown for years! It's no different. And you'll have help! Anna and Geoff do all the online sales, and she'll take care of the inventory. I'm sure Anna can spend a few hours with you in the shop when you need her, and you can close at night until I come back if you want. Please think about it," Ruth pleaded.

Sarah walked around the quilt shop wondering what it would be like to work there. She knew what her hesitation was, but she didn't tell Ruth. Sarah had only been quilting for a couple of years, and she often heard customers asking Ruth questions she would never be able to answer. She wanted to talk about that with Ruth, but she was embarrassed. She knew Ruth would assure her she could handle it, but when it came to quilting, Ruth had far more confidence in her than she had in herself.

She loved being in the shop. There were quilts hanging on every available wall, and the bolts displayed a dazzling rainbow of color when customers stepped into the shop.

"What about the classes?" Sarah asked. "I can't teach classes."

"We can postpone the winter classes, or I can try to find a teacher to come in. Actually, I was wondering if you might want to teach one of the classes you took on the quilting cruise." Sarah had just returned from an exciting Caribbean quilting cruise.

"*Me?*" Sarah wailed. "I'm no teacher."

"I think you would be a great teacher, Sarah, but right now I need you in the shop."

"Let me get back to you tomorrow, Ruth. I know you need to make your plans, so I'll decide quickly. By the way, how's your mother? Have you heard anything?"

"She doesn't have long. She's insisted on staying at home, and I guess that's best. All the hospital can do is prolong her life, and she's ready to go. Papa wanted to be at home, too, but he died in the hospital. That must have felt so alien to him," she added sadly.

Ruth was born Amish and lived in Ohio until she was seventeen. She went away to art school during her *rumspringa*, that time that Amish young people spend outside of their community to make sure they are ready to commit to the Amish way of life. While away, she met Nathan and they were married. Ruth's father rejected them both and, for many years, Ruth lived outside her community and away from her family.

Ruth's mother was not as adamant about it, and now that her husband was gone, she wanted to spend her last days with Ruth, perhaps to make up for lost years.

"I could ask Katie to take a semester off and come work in the shop, but she's doing so well! I just can't bring myself to do that to her."

"Absolutely not, Ruth! Don't do that. Your daughter is exactly where she should be. We'll work this out some way. I want to talk with Charles, and I'll call you in the morning."

"Thank you, Sarah," Ruth said as she hugged her friend. "I appreciate that you would even consider it. I'll talk to you tomorrow."

Sarah left the shop and returned home through the park. It was a cool October afternoon with a bite in the air. She wished she had brought Barney. He loved walking into town, and he was such good company. *If he were with me now, I'd talk this over with him, and he would look at me with his big brown eyes full of love and wag his tail.* Sarah adopted Barney from the Humane Society when she first moved to Cunningham Village. He helped her adjust to life in a retirement community by giving her love, an excuse to go out walking in the neighborhood, and someone to share her new life.

Arriving home, she scratched Barney's ears and opened the back door for him, again feeling thankful she had enclosed the backyard with a fence. She then put in a call to Charles. "How about dinner?" she asked when he answered. He agreed immediately, and they decided to drive into town for Chinese food. She had been seeing Charles for over a year, and it was becoming evident to both of them that this was much more than a friendship. Sarah was aware that Charles was in love with her, but she had been reluctant to face her own feelings. When she lost her husband, Jonathan, she had been devastated, and didn't expect to ever fall in love again. However, if she were honest with herself, she would have to admit that is precisely what had happened. At seventy years old, she was in love!

"Let's go see Sophie," she said to Barney. He jumped up from his spot in the kitchen and ran in a circle before clumsily pulling his leash off the hook and dropping it at Sarah's feet. It wasn't that he understood all of what she said, but the word *go* was enough for him!

They walked across the street to Sophie's house, Barney sniffing the entire way. Despite her raucous personality, Sophie had been Sarah's closest friend and confidant since she moved to the village. Sophie was in her mid-seventies and rotund with a contagious laugh and an endless repertoire of hilarious stories. She also had a heart of gold and was the best friend a person could have.

"Don't bring that flea magnet into my house," Sophie said gruffly as she opened the door.

"Sophie! You know you don't mean that, and you've hurt his feelings!" Sarah responded as they followed her into the living room.

As soon as Sophie was seated, Barney hurried over and put his paws on her lap, looking lovingly into her eyes. She surreptitiously slipped a treat from her pocket, which he appeared to inhale before stretching out across her feet. "His feelings don't look hurt to me," Sophie grumbled. Barney closed his eyes and sighed deeply.

"I can see you managing Stitches," Sophie told Sarah after hearing about Ruth's dilemma, but she didn't have much sympathy for Sarah's fears. "I don't get it! You know how to quilt. You managed Keller's Market for years. Why not manage Running Stitches?"

"You make it sound so simple, Sophie. What if a customer asks me something I don't know?"

"Well, let me see now." Sophie scrunched up her face, held her head, and faked deep concentration for a few moments. She suddenly looked up with surprise and said, "I've got it! You say, 'I don't know!'"

"Oh, Sophie. I guess I'm just scared, and I shouldn't let that stop me."

"… and you could take Barney with you."

"Really?" Sarah responded, brightening up. She hadn't thought of that, but it would be fun having him there with her. Ruth had encouraged her to bring him anytime, and many of the customers had gotten to know him. "I would feel better with him there for some reason."

By the time Charles arrived that evening, Sarah had just about decided to take on the challenge. A few minutes with Charles concluded the debate. She had expected the evening to be about deciding what to do and, instead, it turned out to be a celebration of a new adventure.

A Note
from the Author

I hope you enjoyed *Sea Bound* as much as I enjoyed writing it. This is the third book in A Quilting Cozy series and is followed by *Patchwork Connections*, which finds Charles pulling his cop hat out of storage and hoping to solve a mystery close to Sarah's heart.

On page 213, I have included a preview to *Patchwork Connections* so that you can get an idea of what our cast of characters will be involved in next.

Please let me know how you are enjoying this series. I love hearing from my readers and encourage you to contact me on my blog or send me an email.

Best wishes,

Carol Dean Jones
caroldeanjones.com
quiltingcozy@gmail.com

READER'S GUIDE:
A QUILTING COZY SERIES
by Carol Dean Jones

1. Sarah is elated when Caitlyn expresses interest in learning to quilt. Have you had an opportunity to pass on your skills to a young person? How did that experience make you feel?

2. Sophie had been experiencing falls for several months, but she kept it secret from her family and friends. Why do you think she didn't want anyone to know about her falls?

3. What is it about Sarah that allowed her to go swirling down the water slide despite her fear?

4. The cruise brought Sarah and Charles much closer. How is falling in love at seventy different than at younger ages? Or is it?

5. Discuss how the crime on the ship was accomplished. Do you think this could actually be done? What problems would it present?

6. Did you pick up any clues along the way that lead you to suspect how the book would end?

A Quilting Cozy Series by Carol Dean Jones

Tie Died
a quilting cozy
Carol Dean Jones

Running Stitches
a quilting cozy
Carol Dean Jones

Sea Bound
a quilting cozy
Carol Dean Jones

Patchwork Connections
a quilting cozy
Carol Dean Jones

Stitched Together
a quilting cozy
Carol Dean Jones

Moon Over the Mountain
a quilting cozy
Carol Dean Jones

The Rescue Quilt
a quilting cozy
Carol Dean Jones

Missing Memories
a quilting cozy
Carol Dean Jones

Tattered & Torn
a quilting cozy
Carol Dean Jones

Left Holding the Bag
a quilting cozy
Carol Dean Jones

Beneath Missouri Stars
a quilting cozy
Carol Dean Jones

Frayed Edges
a quilting cozy
Carol Dean Jones